# Fifteen Minutes of Fame

## Three Rivers Ranch Romance™
### Book 14

## Liz Isaacson

ISBN-13: 978-1-63876-344-4

*"A waiting person is a patient person. The word patience means the willingness to stay where we are and live the situation out to the full in the belief that something hidden there will manifest itself to us."*

Henri J.M. Nouwen

# Chapter One

Navy Richards drew in a deep breath as the ticket attendant made his way toward her. He seemed nice, fatherly, probably bored to death. He punched tickets and made small talk, but Navy didn't feel any of the man's calm energy. She gripped her ticket to Three Rivers, Texas for all she was worth, wondering for the hundredth time if she'd decided correctly.

*Yes*, she thought, reassuring herself for the hundred and first time. She needed a break from her insane job as a pediatric nurse. Needed a break from the dozens of dating apps she had uninstalled just the previous night. Needed a break from her perfect younger sister, her gorgeous husband, and their new baby—which Navy had helped deliver and then care for while her sister sat in the hospital bed like a celebrity.

Familiar jealousy, bitterness, and frustration rose

through her throat, and Navy didn't like it. She didn't want to feel that way about her only sister. About anyone. She'd prayed more often than she'd doubted her decision to take the leave of absence and move hundreds of miles away for six months.

Her feelings would subside for a few days, and then they came back—seemingly stronger and louder than before.

"Ticket?"

Navy pulled herself from her thoughts and extended her ticket toward the attendant. She had to force her fingers to loosen so he could take it and punch it. He didn't linger with her, didn't ask her why she was going to Three Rivers—a small speck of a city—on a bus, didn't ask her how long she was staying. A sting started behind her heart, and Navy sighed as she leaned her head against the window and watched the Texas wilderness roll by.

She couldn't help her fantasies of finding and marrying a good man. She'd been working hard at it, going out with everyone who asked, signing up for every available dating app, kept as many evenings free as possible. At this point, she'd probably been out with every available bachelor in Austin.

"Time for a change," she whispered to her faint reflection in the glass. And so what if the change she wanted included a matchmaker? Why did Lexie get to dictate to Navy how she found her perfect catch? But her younger sister had definitely had plenty to say about Navy's decision to travel to Three Rivers and meet with an eighty-three-year-old matchmaker. None of it was nice. Or supportive. Or what Navy wanted to hear.

After all, not everyone could get married, live in a quaint brick home with a white picket fence, and have a baby whenever they wanted by age twenty-eight. Oh, no. Navy was several years older than that and had practically handed Lexie her husband on a silver platter.

She eradicated the thought of Scott before it could sour her mood further. She drew in another breath, prepared for anything once she arrived in Three Rivers.

Eight hours and two very stiff legs later, Navy disembarked from the bus in Three Rivers, Texas. The night air tasted wonderful. She turned in a circle, drinking in the bright lights of the bus station and the way she felt so *free* here.

Navy beamed at the park across the street, but it darkness didn't offer her a particularly nice welcome. Maybe coming here to meet with a matchmaker *was* a dumb idea. But it could also incite the change Navy needed in her life. Legend or not. Myth or not. Fantasy or fact. Navy didn't care. She believed in the magic of this place, and she wasn't going to let Lexie's poisoned lectures influence her.

The bus rumbled away, leaving Navy alone on the sidewalk, all of her bags with her. Reality descended, and she put on her backpack, shouldered her purse and then another bag, and tilted the wheeled suitcase behind her. The fact that she could fit her whole life into a few bags had surprised and saddened her, but now she felt liberated. She crossed the street without looking for traffic, because it seemed the downtown area where she'd arrived had already closed for the evening.

As she arrived at the fountain, she did notice one establishment with bright lights still on. The restaurant also boasted loud country music when the front doors opened and a couple spilled onto the street. They didn't glance in her direction, and in the next moment, the lights dimmed and left Navy to herself.

The stories about how women came here to find their true love had given Navy more hope than she'd had in five years. And that couple? Maybe it was a sign that she'd find her happily-ever-after in this place she'd never dreamed of visiting.

Her own aunt had convinced her that the trip to Three Rivers was warranted. She'd found her husband after a meeting with the very person Navy had an appointment with the following day. She looked around the park, imagining the tea lights her aunt had detailed, the summer dances that brought out all the cowboys from the nearby ranches.

Navy sighed, thinking maybe she'd meet the just-right man for her too, somewhere in Austin in a park like this, after her meeting tomorrow morning.

A smile stole across Navy's face, and she unburdened herself from her baggage. She cast a quick glance around to see if anyone was watching. She didn't think nine-thirty was late, but apparently for this small town, and it being a weeknight, it was.

She twirled and danced her way down the sidewalk, a low hum in the back of her throat. A sense of wonderment and magic infected her, and she just knew tonight was the first night of the rest of her life. That she'd just finally done something to find the right person.

A gasp of desperation ended her dance and she stilled next to her suitcases. She didn't want millions of dollars. She didn't need a big mansion. She spent fifty hours a week cradling and caring for babies, and she wanted one of her own. She wanted a husband to gaze at her with so much love, the way the new dads did in labor and delivery. They could live in a basement for all she cared.

*Please let this work,* she said to the stars before bending and collecting her belongings. She'd told the people she was renting a cottage from she'd be there by ten, and she had a few blocks to walk before arriving.

*Thank you, she thought through every step. Thank you for giving me this opportunity in Three Rivers, Texas.*

THE FOLLOWING MORNING further proved to Navy that she'd moved into a shack. Last night, the darkness had obscured the grime, the fact that the linoleum cracked in front of the stove and peeled where it met the carpet.

She'd rented the "cottage" from natives of Three

Rivers for further luck in her quest to find a husband. The Shepherd's had met her on the front porch and helped her carry her bags out to the cottage, which sat in a corner of their large, impressive yard. A rutted dirt lane led back to the cottage, and Navy needed to find some mode of transportation besides her feet.

Or maybe she wouldn't. She had her laptop, and the cottage did have electricity and Internet, so she was pretty set. She wasn't planning to work while in town, as she'd only be here for six months. Really, she needed an escape from her life, a vacation to reset herself. So that when she returned to Austin she'd be ready to be the kind of woman a man couldn't resist.

She left the cottage and it's lukewarm showers in favor of the late March Texas sunshine. Nothing could ruin today. Because today, Navy was meeting with Nancy Redd, the matchmaker who had promised Aunt Izzie that she'd marry a cowboy and live on a ranch. Navy wasn't sure if ranch life was what she wanted, necessarily, but she believed Nancy could give her a push in the right direction.

Aunt Izzie and Uncle Marvin had lived here in Three Rivers for about a decade after their wedding. Then they'd moved to Wimberley, a small town about an hour west of Austin, to be closer to family. Uncle Marvin had worked at Three Rivers Ranch, which Navy's cousin Heidi owned.

As she approached the address she'd been given,

Navy's heart pounded with anticipation. Her footsteps slowed as she contemplated what Nancy would tell her. Her throat turned dry at the horrifying thought that perhaps there wasn't a match for her on this earth.

The house came into view, and it was obviously well kept. Clipped, green grass went right up to the street, where a mailbox stood straight and strong. A two-story house in pale blue boasted a bright red star above the front window. Rose bushes lined the sidewalk to the porch and along the front of the house. The only thing that seemed out of place was a birdhouse that looked like it had been put together by a bottle of Elmer's glue, a vat of popsicle sticks, and gallons of finger paint.

She gave the ugly lawn decoration a wary glance. Something drew her toward it and she stepped across the grass to examine it further. It sat up between a rose bush bearing peachy-colored blossoms and one with pink the color of lemonade. She couldn't quite reach the birdhouse, but she didn't really want to touch it.

"You like that birdhouse?"

Navy spun toward the masculine voice and took in the form of a man several inches taller than her and wide enough to block the sun. He wore a cowboy hat the color of graphite and a dark beard salted with loads of gray. Instant attraction sprang through her system at his maturity, at the scent of his cologne as it stuck in the air surrounding them.

He watched her with a pair of dark, dangerous eyes, clearly waiting for something.

She jolted to attention as embarrassment rushed to her face, heating it to the color of the red roses at the end of the line. "Oh, the birdhouse." She looked at the hideous thing again. "It's...did their grandson make it?"

He tilted his head to the side, confusion evident in his expression. "What do you mean?"

"It's crafty."

"Crafty?"

Navy got the impression that she'd said all the wrong things. "It looks...unique."

He crossed his arms, which only served to make his muscles that much more impressive. "It *is* unique. One of a kind, in fact."

"That's a relief." Navy added a short burst of laughter to her statement in an attempt to smooth things over with this man. "Well, I have an appointment, so I should get going." She hooked her thumb over her shoulder and backed away from the man for a few steps before turning around completely.

She felt the weight of his stare on her back, but she hadn't come here to impress a surly cowboy with strange questions about a clearly dysfunctional birdhouse.

No, she'd come here to find her soul mate, and there was only one person who could help her do that. So with a determined breath, she rounded the house and entered the door on the side, just as instructed.

# Chapter Two

Gavin Redd watched the blonde disappear around the side of his grandparents' house, her words still echoing in his head. *Unique. Unique. Unique.*

What did that mean?

He glanced at the birdhouse, that yes, their grandson had made. Somehow he'd known not to say that *he* was the grandson, and oh, that he was forty years old.

He yanked the birdhouse from the roses. His grandfather hadn't even seen it yet, so it wouldn't matter if Gavin took it back to his shop for a little more work. He passed the side entrance to his grandmother's matchmaking studio, where the blonde had gone. His stomach twisted. How women could believe in that stuff escaped his understanding. He shook his head as the door closed, hoping his grandmother would let this woman down gently. No one had complained about anything his grandmother had done, but she was getting up there in years now, and Gavin wanted her to stop the whole matchmaking thing.

The fact that he didn't believe in it didn't help. But it didn't matter what he didn't believe in. The matchmaking had seen his grandparents through some tough times, and still paid several of their bills.

*Your bills*, he reminded himself as he retreated to the house next door, which his grandparents also owned and allowed him to live in rent-free. He earned his keep, to be sure. He mowed. Watered. Raked. Gardened. Now that the weather was turning warm again, his work outside would only increase.

He generally enjoyed the time he spent in the yard and gardens with his grandfather, who adored roses and tomatoes above all other plants. He liked smiling at Grandmother as she rocked on the front porch and brought out pitchers of sweet tea and plates of cookies for when they needed a break.

Gavin kept their house in good repair too, had adopted both of their dogs as his own, and generally made sure they were in good health and good spirits. He'd been taking care of them for a decade, and something gnawed at him in quiet moments like these.

He entered his house and closed the door behind him, the birdhouse still clenched in his fist. He paused for a moment and allowed his thoughts to settle, gave himself a moment to breathe. And he knew his time here in Three Rivers was nearly over.

Well, maybe not completely. But on this parcel of land. With these chores. There was something else out there for him, but the problem was, he didn't know what. Or where it would be.

With his Big Four-Oh Birthday last month, Gavin needed to start building his own life, and he'd wanted a ranch for as long as he could remember. He'd worked at the B&B for a while, but they'd fallen on hard times and couldn't afford to pay him what he was worth. Three Rivers, the biggest operating ranch in the area, was full-up at the moment. And Sterling Springs Ranch was a ranch only because the sign said so. It wasn't an operational ranch anymore, and he wasn't interested in using his ranch management degree to oversee destination weddings.

No, sir. Gavin wanted a big homestead, with cowboys living on-site, and acres and acres of land for cattle and horses and chickens. Maybe a few sheep. He wanted a wide open sky and a Texas breeze rolling across the countryside.

There were ranches out there to be bought, but nothing in Gavin's preferred location—near his family here—and within his budget. Admittedly, he didn't have much, but he'd known men who'd bought ranches with less than he had.

He set about cleaning up his breakfast from that morning, then took the lopsided birdhouse into the wood shop behind his house. He stared at it for several long seconds, trying to decide what the woman had seen in it.

Trying to decide why he cared what she'd thought. She had beautiful blue eyes, and long hair the color of his favorite corn grits down at the diner. Her skin looked like she spent most of her time indoors. Either that, or she wore an excessive amount of sunscreen when she went outside.

*Nope, definitely an indoor type of woman*, he thought as he picked up a hammer and pulled out a couple of errant nails. The whole birdhouse collapsed after that, leaving Gavin with a pile of wood at his feet, wondering how a couple of nails had held the whole thing together.

He chuckled. No wonder the woman had been staring at it with such a look of abhorrence on her face. He'd stared at her for a good half a minute before going over to her, almost drawn to her like a magnet to metal.

He shook his head and opened his phone. He could find a video online that would help him repair the birdhouse. Anything to drive a complete stranger from his mind.

Gavin knew most people in Three Rivers, and newcomers usually only stayed a week at most. Long enough to visit the touristy attractions, maybe get hitched themselves, or to pass through on their way to southern Hill Country, where more rivers and prettier countryside existed.

He didn't have much patience for tourists, and even less for the women who came here looking for love. The town wasn't quite big enough to provide matches for every female wanting one, and thankfully, his grandmother had taken to matching people with the type of man they should be looking for, not an actual man from Three Rivers.

Truth be told, Gavin didn't trust anyone who'd listen to his grandmother for dating advice. He found them desperate and somewhat delusional to think someone could really give them what they needed just by spending a few minutes with them and asking a few questions.

The blonde woman flashed through his mind as he set a blue-painted board against a red one. She certainly didn't need help getting a date. Someone as beautiful as her probably went out with a new guy every night.

Blue, Gavin's yellow Lab, nosed his way into the shop, bringing Misfit and Miles with him. The dogs roamed as a pack, Blue their leader, across the three-acre property his grandparents owned. Blue flopped at Gavin's feet, right on top of several pieces of wood he still needed to fit back together.

"Go get a drink, lazy bones." Gavin nudged the dog with his toe, and Blue moved to the corner where fresh water waited. Misfit sniffed Gavin's boots, the way the pug always did. And Miles, a huge black Newfoundland, stood guard at the door.

Gavin put the birdhouse back together and stepped away from it to evaluate. It still looked like someone had mashed wet wood together with their bare hands and tried to shape it into something resembling a birdhouse.

Unwilling to put it back in the front yard for more strangers to comment on, Gavin left it in the shop and decided to go see what Grandmother had made for breakfast.

He opened his door and plowed right into the blonde from earlier. She yelped and tried to get her feet out from under his, only succeeding in tripping him further. He grabbed onto her arms and managed to keep both of them upright.

"Whoa," he said like she was a steed.

With them both settled and staring at each other, he asked, "What are you doin' here?" His grandmother had tried to set him up a half-dozen times with her clients before he'd told her he was off the market permanently. He wasn't really, but for her clients, he most certainly was. If she'd sent this woman over here....

"Your grandmother—"

Gavin growled.

"Let me finish." The woman cocked her hip and splayed one hand on it. Her pink-painted nails didn't escape his attention. Neither did her lithe frame and gentle curves. He yanked his eyes back to hers, a flush rising through his body in an uncomfortable way. He hadn't dated in a couple of years, and he certainly wasn't interested in another blonde.

If only his pulse would stop jumping and settle back into his chest.

"Your grandmother said you're handy. I told her I was living in this run-down cottage—it's a shack really, and *that's* being generous—and it needs a lot of work. She suggested that you might could do the job."

Gavin blocked the inside of the shop with his body. He didn't want her to see the birdhouse or any other evidence of his handiness. "What kind of work?"

"Oh, you know." The woman waved her hand like she was swatting away an annoying fly. "Some painting, and some flooring that isn't properly adhered. Maybe something with the hot water heater. That kind of stuff."

"Where are you staying?"

"In Gerry and Olivia Shepherd's outbuilding."

Gavin's eyebrows rose. "The Shepherd's, huh? You've done some research on the history of Three Rivers, is that it?"

She bristled, and Gavin realized a bit too late how arctic his tone had sounded. "Never mind. I'm sure I can find someone else to help me." She turned to leave, which sent relief and disappointment diving through Gavin at the same time. He couldn't make sense of how he felt, and it had been a long time since that had happened.

"I'm not sure I'd want to hire you anyway," she called over her shoulder. "I've seen the houses you make for birds."

By the time he'd processed what she'd said, she'd

disappeared down the street. He walked to the front lawn and glanced north and then south, where he found her already a good half a block away. The woman could *stride*, he'd give her that much.

She also hadn't missed the fact that *he* had constructed the birdhouse. Poorly, too.

Still, he wanted to know her name, and why she'd come to Three Rivers if not to fulfill her silly fantasies. Usually a woman didn't stay in town long if she'd only come to get her match. But this woman had rented somewhere to live, as if she was planning to stay.

He glanced back to his grandmother's matchmaking entrance. She'd tell him everything he wanted to know about the mysterious woman. All he'd have to do is mention that he forgot to get her name and he needed to call her about the cottage at the Shepherd's.

He'd taken one step to go ask when he faltered. If he involved Grandmother at all, he'd have to answer questions from now until Christmas. Maybe longer.

And he didn't need that drama in his life. He knew almost everyone in town. He could figure things out with a few texts and spare himself the constant badgering. With that decision made, he went back inside to fetch the dogs. They all needed a run before the morning got too hot.

He pushed open the door and heard a crunch-crunch-crunch sound. "Blue," he chastised. The dog looked up from a pile of splintered wood that used to be Gavin's birdhouse. Misfit whined, and Miles hadn't moved from his position just inside the door. He barked, his warning about Blue way too late.

Gavin entered the shop and pulled the half-chewed piece of wood from his dog's mouth. "We don't eat birdhouses."

Blue looked at him with a quizzical expression in his eyes, his ears at attention and his head cocked as if to say, *That was a birdhouse?*

# Chapter Three

*You should be looking for an Aquarius.*

The matchmaker's words rotated through Navy's mind for the rest of the day. She'd found the perfect patch of shade on the north side of the cottage where a lounge chair had been positioned, seemingly just for her. She'd brought out her phone and her tablet, but she'd barely looked at them.

*You're a Libra, and very spontaneous and fun. Don't be so worried about being popular. Don't worry about having a classy man on your arm.*

Navy had sat in her chair, surprise and shock jolting through her with every word the white-haired woman had said. She'd possessed kind eyes and a calm spirit, but she spoke with the authority of someone who'd made many successful matches over many years.

Navy had drank in every word, and she'd listened to them again a half a dozen times since then.

"Enjoy your time here," her phone's recorder played back. "Don't worry too much about the future."

There had been a lot of advice dispensed. Near the end of her hour-long appointment, Navy had finally plucked up the courage to ask, "Will I find the right man for me?"

"Certainly," Nancy had proclaimed without a moment's hesitation. "You have a good sense of who you are. What you need now is the confidence to be yourself. Once you do that, the right man will come into your life."

Navy paused the recording and leaned her head back. A soft breeze blew across her face as she contemplated Nancy's words.

She'd never felt like she wasn't confident. She knew what she was doing at work. She was an excellent nurse who kept calm in difficult and stressful situations. She could soothe any baby. She knew she had a certain affect on men, what with her light blonde hair and full lips she kept painted a shiny pink.

*Except for Gavin....*

The thought drifted across her mind, unbidden. Why she'd thought of him, she didn't know. Nancy had spent a few minutes bragging about her grandson when Navy had complimented the yard. She'd also spilled the beans that he'd made the birdhouse Navy had insulted.

Her earlier embarrassment returned, but she stuffed it

away after a moment. The man hadn't exactly been nice when she'd asked him about his services, and how was she supposed to know he'd built the birdhouse? It literally looked like a five-year-old had done it.

An image of the cottage flashed through her mind, and Navy thought that even a five-year-old could improve it. She needed to ask the Shepherd's if they'd mind if she did a few home renovations first anyway, so she let her thoughts of Gavin drift away on the wind.

LATER THAT NIGHT, she pushed through the front doors of The Horseshoe Bar & Grill, having been informed by their website that they served fries by the basketful and offered dancing and live music every night. Being Friday, Navy wanted to get a feel for the night life in this town— and she wasn't disappointed.

The music blared from a stage in the back of the restaurant, where four men played instruments. Piano, bass, fiddle, and guitar. They all wore jeans with belt buckles the size of dinner plates. Blue and white plaid shirts and white cowboy hats completed the look.

A sucker for a man playing a guitar, Navy grinned.

"Just you tonight?" The woman standing in front of her wore short shorts and a red T-shirt that was tied on the side for a reason Navy couldn't fathom.

"Just me," she said, trying to remember the last time

she'd gone out by herself. She couldn't, because Navy never went out by herself. If she wasn't going to dinner with a date, she got together with a group of nurses. She thrived on the social aspect of things, and though the hostess seated her in a booth by herself, the atmosphere of the bar indicated that she wasn't really alone.

She ordered the bottomless fries and three dipping sauces, along with a hefty diet soda, before asking the waitress, a woman named Candy with auburn hair, "Do you live here in Three Rivers?"

"Yep, born and raised."

"So can I ask you a question?"

"Shoot."

"If I needed someone to do some home repairs, who would I hire?"

Candy grinned. "I thought it was going to be a hard one. But that's easy. Gavin Redd. He can do everything." She moved to the next table, and Navy let the words roll around in her head.

*He can do everything. Everything.*

*Everything?*

Navy's thoughts deviated into fantasies before she could turn her attention back to the band. A flush rose through her neck, making her hot and the air conditioner seem defunct. The band had moved on to a slower song, but no one danced in the open area between the tables and the stage. Navy supposed it was a little early for that.

She'd have to be blind not to notice the way several

men orbited her table, but she didn't make eye contact with any of them. She enjoyed her fries, determined to do exactly as Nancy had suggested and find her confidence before searching for a man.

Since she wasn't planning on staying in Three Rivers permanently, there was no reason for her to jump the gun and start looking already. Besides, she needed time to figure out how to ask someone's birthday before committing to a date with them. Because she was done wasting her time. Once she had all the tools she needed, she planned to hit the dating scene with a vengeance. And that meant only going out with Aquarius's.

Just as the country line dance party started, the front doors opened again. They'd been opening and closing for an hour, but Navy hadn't glanced at them once. Now, though, it seemed like the entire restaurant paused, and Navy's attention swung to the man who had just walked in.

Gavin Redd.

Her heart shot out an extra beat. Then two.

*Was he an Aquarius?*

She shook her head to dislodge the thought. He wasn't available, that much had been clear from their conversations that morning. In fact, she'd gotten a cold vibe from him both times, and she went back to the last of her food.

"More fries?" Candy asked, picking up the nearly empty basket.

"What the heck?" Navy glanced up. "Can I have the sweet potato ones this time?"

"Sure thing." She moved away, once again giving Navy a clear sightline to Gavin. He glanced in her direction too, doing a double-take before his gaze truly settled on hers.

He scowled—actually *scowled*—before turning back to the cash register with a To-Go sign above it.

Of course he wouldn't come in and grace the restaurant with his presence. *He probably just doesn't want to sit alone*, Navy told herself as she focused on the band. She wasn't a mean-spirited person. There was just something about him that riled her.

And now that she knew she could get her fries to go, she might do the same next time. The song ended, and she clapped along with everyone else. As the band started up again, she glanced back at Gavin.

He was gone, and her chest pinched a little. In the next moment, she caught sight of him walking toward her. Her heart froze as if someone had dropped it into liquid nitrogen. It struggled against the ice surrounding it, and then burst free, the beat now rapid and intense.

Especially when he stepped to the end of her table and asked, "Mind if I join you?" He didn't wait for her to answer before sliding onto the bench across from her. Every eye seemed to follow him, which meant he had a story.

And Navy really wanted to know what it was.

So she smiled and though it wasn't necessary, said, "Sure, have a seat."

He smiled too, a quick gesture that barely lasted long enough for her to notice the dimple in his left cheek. But she did, because Navy was trained to notice everything. Every little hiccup. Every sound a newborn made. Every sign of distress from a mother who'd just gone through a difficult labor.

Gavin opened his Styrofoam container and said, "I love their buffalo sliders here." He lifted one out and offered it to her.

Navy normally would've passed. She barely knew this man. Scratch that. She didn't know him at all. "Buffalo?" she said, reaching for the neat little package of food. "Never had it."

He pulled the slider back. "You've got to tell me your name first."

She blinked at him. "Oh." She giggled and leaned onto her elbows. "It's Navy Richards."

"I'm sure my grandmother told you who I am."

"She did, yes."

He passed her the slider and took one out for himself. They bit into them together, and the flavor of onion, pickle, and the game meat exploded in her mouth. She moaned and finished off the slider in only one more bite. As she wiped her hands, she nodded. "I see why you like those. Delicious."

"What else did Grandmother tell you about me?"

"Nothing." Navy watched him for his reaction. "I mentioned that the place I was renting was in disrepair, and she said you'd built that birdhouse—" She muted her voice as his eyes took on that stormy quality again. "Forget it."

He glared at her for a solid minute. Long enough for Candy to bring her fries and take her soda glass to be refilled. Candy had just set it on the table and disappeared again when Gavin said, "That was my first attempt at a birdhouse, I'll have you know."

She dipped her sweet potato fry in garlic aioli. "So you must be better with a real house. You know, fixing walls and stuff."

"I get by."

Navy eyed him, but didn't stare openly. He ate the rest of his sliders and his regular fries while she enjoyed her second basket of fried food. He did more than "get by." She'd asked Olivia Shepherd if she could do a few repairs, and Olivia had recommended Gavin. So had Candy, just a few minutes ago. So why had that birdhouse looked like road kill?

Would her cottage look the same if she asked Gavin to come repair the walls, paint, and maybe do something about that water heater? Maybe she'd be showering in ice the next time she stepped into the tiny stall. *Ice and snakes*, she thought. *Ain't Texas grand?*

He didn't offer to come over. Didn't ask her any questions. Just took up space across from her and ate his food while the band played and the dance floor filled up.

When he finished, she asked, "Do you dance?"

A strange look crossed his face—another part of his story—which he closed down quickly. He sighed as he leaned back into the booth. "I used to. Now, these old boots don't do much dancin'."

Navy found his twang adorable and told herself to stop. She'd not used her ticket to Three Rivers to find a groom.

She had *not*.

Even if he was sexy, and could pound an entire container of fries, and could possibly wield a hammer and fix all her problems.

Well, her physical living condition problems anyway.

# Chapter Four

Gavin's toe bounced to the song The Wheat Stalks played. Yes, he knew the band. Yes, he knew all the members in the band. Yes, he'd danced to their songs before. With another blonde woman.

He didn't really want to repeat that chapter in his life —because it was like an entire volume. Years, wasted.

All so Joan Young could meet with his grandmother behind closed doors, deem him unworthy to be her soul mate, and head off for the greener fields of Dallas. He'd never really had a problem with the Bride legend until then.

He could still feel the heat from her touch as she pressed her palm against his bicep. "We're not meant to be."

The wispy quality of her voice had annoyed him then. Now it made him angry too.

Meant to be? What did that even mean?

Gavin had gone out onto the open range that night, almost two years ago. He'd never hated something as much as he had while staring at the stars. And the problem was, he didn't even know what he hated.

He'd stopped trying after that. Every giggling girl who came through town wasn't looking for *him*. No, they thought Prince Wonderful existed somewhere out there for them, and they had to come to Three Rivers to figure out where. None of them ever thought there might be a man right there, right in front of them, the right one if they'd only give him a chance.

And Navy Richards was no different.

At least he knew her name now. But he wasn't going to dance with her. Even coming over and sitting down had surely alerted the gossips. They'd be the talk of the town for the next week, until something more interesting happened where the locals at the diner or the hair salon could be witnesses.

Gavin stood, taking his trash with him. "Well, I best be off. Nice to finally know your name, Navy."

She slid out of the booth too, like she might leave with him. Pure panic pounded through his bloodstream, and he stared at her until she fell back to the vinyl bench. He nodded once, pressed his cowboy hat further onto his head, and strode out of the restaurant. Alone.

Just the way he liked it.

He'd made it to his truck before he admitted he didn't

really want to be alone. He just didn't want her to walk out with him. Didn't like being forty and the talk of the town. No, sir. Gavin didn't need that.

Now, if Navy's cornflower blue eyes would stop haunting him, he might be able to see well enough to get back to his house.

* * *

THE NEXT DAY, Gavin woke to the sound of his phone ringing. The sun had barely lit the world, so he scrambled to pick up the call, his heart skipping around his chest. Was it one of his grandparents?

The screen said Squire Ackerman, and Gavin's pulse switched from one of fear to one of anticipation.

"Morning, Squire," he said, sitting up and rubbing his free hand through his hair.

"Hope I didn't wake you."

"No, nope." Gavin stifled a yawn. A cowboy like Squire probably slept standing up, if he slept at all.

"Great. Wondering if you have time to come out to the ranch sometime today."

Gavin had a contracted job at Sterling Springs Ranch to fix an arch that had blown over in a windstorm last week. He wasn't quite sure what was the difference between a wedding arch and a birdhouse, except for the fact that he could construct one of them. In fact, he'd built all the arches at Sterling Ranch, no problem.

He could fix walls, and floors, and roofs. But apparently, he couldn't make a birdhouse that would gain anyone's trust.

Didn't matter. No one was calling him to make birdhouses. He was simply dabbling in his shop during the slower winter months. But now that the weather was flipping to summer—in Texas there was hot and then hotter—he'd had more work, especially at the destination wedding venue of Sterling Ranch.

"You still there?" Squire asked, and Gavin startled.

"Yes," he said quickly. "Just looking at my schedule. I could come out after lunch."

"That should be fine."

"What's goin' on?" Gavin asked, setting his feet on the floor and burrowing them under the warm body of Blue.

"I'm wondering if you're still looking for a cowboy job." Squire's voice gave nothing away.

But excitement paraded through Gavin. "Yeah, of course. "I mean, yes. Yes, sir."

Squire chuckled and said, "Gavin, you're older than me. Don't call me sir. Just come by my office when you get here. If I'm not here, someone will radio me."

Gavin pressed his eyes closed. "Okay, see you this afternoon." He hung up and wondered if he'd already made a fool of himself. He was a year older than Squire, but the man owned the largest and most successful cattle ranch within hundreds of miles.

An inaudible sigh passed through his body. If he could

get a permanent position at Three Rivers Ranch.... Just the thought had hope soaring through his body. He had a good life. A good life worth living. He didn't need a wife or a sprawling homestead to achieve happiness, but a real position on a ranch would be welcome.

*The pastor's latest sermon crossed his mind. Do not linger on the storms of life. Do not spend time wishing and waiting for what might be. Choose to be happy now.*

Gavin had been choosing. Choosing to be happy as he drove nails into wood and remade the arch into something substantial and beautiful. Choosing to be happy though he hadn't achieved his dreams of owning his own ranch. Choosing to be happy right where God had put him and kept him all these years.

Hours later, with the arch fixed at one ranch, and his truck headed north of town toward Three Rivers Ranch, his phone rang, and he glanced at the unfamiliar number. He went ahead and answered it with a "Hello?"

"Did you know there's not a single person in this town that will recommend anyone but you to fix up my cottage?"

"Navy?"

"I've asked six different people. *Six.* The answer's always the same. Gavin Redd. Gavin Redd. Gavin— *Redd.*" She didn't sound happy about that.

He didn't know how to respond, so he just let her keep talking.

"So I finally asked for your number, and now I'm

asking you to come over and do a little walk-through…or whatever it is you do to tell me what you'd do to fix up this shack and how much it will cost."

Gavin warred with himself. He wanted to turn around and head over right now. He knew where the cottage was; no address needed. At the same time, he didn't want to get involved with women who mocked his birdhouses, visited his grandmother for dating advice, and came to town for an undetermined amount of time.

*You'll be here for an undetermined amount of time*, he reminded himself. A brick fell out of his defensive wall. "How do you know I'm even available?"

"Oh, I don't. In fact, I'm sure you're booked for months, but I thought I'd ask. I'll even pick up some of those sliders from The Stable."

Gavin wasn't booked for months, but Navy didn't need to know that. If he got the job at Three Rivers, he might not have time though. "I like the regular French fries," he said. "None of those sweet potato things."

"They're actually very good."

"I'll take your word for it."

"Regular fries," she confirmed. "So you'll come tonight?"

He wondered how long he'd be out at the ranch, as it was already one-thirty. And with the forty-five minute drive between town and ranch…. "Can I let you know?"

On her end of the line, a horse whinnied. She did not seem like the type to appreciate large mammals in her personal space, though she was clearly from Texas, what with her sexy accent.

"Sure." She wore a smile in her words, and ended the call with an upbeat, not awkward at all, "See you tonight, Gavin."

The call ended just like that, and he stared at his phone, the sound of his name in Navy's voice like music to his ears. He swallowed, sure he was starting to feel soft things for another blonde woman. He couldn't allow that. Wouldn't.

So he'd call and cancel in a couple of hours, claiming his job at the ranch had run long and he couldn't possibly make it to her cottage that evening.

Surely the Lord would forgive the little lie if it protected Gavin's heart. Wouldn't He?

Gavin had shelved Navy by the time he turned off the highway and headed down the dirt road toward the ranch. An entire community existed out here, with two homesteads, two families living and working on the land, the therapeutic riding facility and now a champion horse breeding operation too.

Dozens of trucks could be seen as he rounded the bend, and he had the strong desire to add his to the mix. He didn't need to park at the horse training or healing buildings. No, he turned right and headed for the end of the road, where a large metal structure marked the administration offices for Three Rivers.

Gavin had been here several times before, as the ranch

often needed temporary workers. He caught sight of the cabins through the gaps between barns and other buildings and wondered if there was an opening in one of them for him.

Could he bring his dogs? He knew he couldn't bring his grandparents and he mentally calculated a trip to town and back, checking on them, and possibly eating dinner with them every night like he was used to.

After all, breakfast would be out, though he usually went next door by seven to see what Grandmother had put together for the morning meal.

At least a couple of hours. Probably more.

His heart turned over as he parked way down on the end, the only available spot. A fence sat only a few feet away, but he'd left enough room for someone to get by if they needed to.

He climbed out of the truck, noticing something electric in the air.

Something was wrong.

"Ho!" someone yelled, and Gavin spun, trying to find the source of the sound.

A horse—a very fast, galloping horse—barreled toward him, a woman clinging to the saddle.

Time slowed down, and Gavin had a split second to see so many things. The several men on horses behind the woman. The wild look in the horse's eyes, and the very dust itself lifting into the air.

Someone yelled something, but Gavin didn't hear what and certainly didn't have time to process it.

He jumped in front of the horse, blocking the only escape between his truck and the bullpen. He waved his arms above his head, hoping to make himself look bigger so the horse would stop.

He was not expecting the animal to swing wildly to his left to skirt the bullpen—and head for the wide open range with Navy on his back.

*Navy.*

Gavin saw the terror in his eyes, and the prompted him to *act*. He leapt onto the bottom rung of the fence and climbed it quickly, somehow stepped across the top of the fence like he was a gymnast on the balance beam, and launched himself onto the horse's back as it passed him.

Pain shot through his forty-year-old back, and he grunted. It took several strides of the horse for him to find the rhythm, and by then, he had both arms around Navy.

"It's okay," he yelled, fumbling for the reins. "Do you have the reins?"

She didn't answer, which Gavin took as a no. He leaned in close to her to keep his balance, his mind running as wildly as this horse.

# Chapter Five

Navy clung to the saddle horn for dear life. Behind her, Gavin didn't seem to be doing anything. What was the point of vaulting onto the back of the horse? Obviously she didn't have control of it and couldn't hand him the reins he'd asked for.

She felt a vibration coming from his chest, and she thought he was humming.

"Whoa," he said and went promptly back to humming. She could hear the hoofbeats of the horses behind them, see men fanning out to corral the wayward horse where they wanted it.

But Gavin needed to stop this animal before it hurt himself or a human being. "What's the horse's name?" he asked Navy.

"Charcoal," she managed to say, and Gavin used the

name, stretching past her and hooking his fingers under the headpiece and pulling.

"Whoa there, Charcoal," he said in a commanding voice, adding a hum to the end of the sentence.

Miraculously, the horse slowed.

"There you go," Gavin said. "Good boy, Charcoal. Let's walk." He clicked with his mouth somehow, and the giant equine slowed further. His sides heaved, and Navy didn't let an inch of her grip slip. She was not going to fall off this horse in front of Gavin.

She was not.

Gavin kept humming as the horse moved into a trot and then a walk. He eased his body away from her, and though the afternoon sun was incredibly warm, Navy felt a chill take the place where Gavin's chest used to press against her back.

Before she could fully straighten her spine, cowboys surrounded them. The horse stopped and someone helped her down. Pete, the owner of Courage Reins where Navy had come to ride for a couple of hours, stood right in front of her, concern etched in every line of his face.

"You okay?"

Squire Ackerman, the owner of the ranch where her uncle had worked for a decade, stepped in front of Pete, almost forcing Navy back. "Yes, tell us where you're hurt."

"I'm not hurt," she managed to say. She felt strange among all these tall cowboys, and she glanced around to find Gavin. He stood back a ways, talking with a couple of other men wearing cowboy hats. None of them looked at her.

"You're not hurt?" Pete said, glancing at Squire. "What happened with the horse?"

"He freaked out," Navy said, trying to find something solid to attach her thoughts to. "I don't know what happened."

"Snakes," Squire said in a dark tone, and he turned away.

"There wasn't a loud noise?" Pete asked. He reached out and touched her as if he was sure she'd shatter with the whisper-light touch.

"No," Navy said. "We were going along just fine, headed back." Her legs hurt. Her head pounded like that horse's hooves. She closed her eyes, trying to remember. "We came up to the fence line, and the horse nickered. Whined, you know, made a noise."

"Mm hm," Pete said noncommittally. "And?"

"And then he just bolted." Looking back. Navy was grateful he'd headed toward the ranch and not out into the wild. Who knows if she would've ever been found then?

Pete put his hand on her shoulder. "I think you should get checked out."

"I'm fine," she said, but no one seemed to hear her. Squire and Pete drove her into town to the emergency room, and she couldn't get out of it no matter what she said.

So she suffered through the questions and the probing

and the x-rays, steadfastly proclaiming that she was fine. The doctor came back in with her films and slapped them up on the lightbox.

"You've got a hairline fracture in your left hand," he said, glancing at her. "Is that new?"

Navy started rubbing the damaged limb. "It must be." It didn't hurt, and she told him so.

"No, it's not serious. Can you think of how you got it?" He flipped off the lightbox.

"I have no idea." She had been gripping the saddle horn pretty hard. Had she fractured her hand with a tight grip? How ridiculous would that be?

She took in a deep breath, the stale, sterile scent of the hospital soothing her somehow. This was her familiar place. Something she knew well.

"Well, I can prescribe some painkillers." He leaned against a cabinet and nodded to the nurse, who started tapping on a keyboard. "I imagine you're a bit shook up and probably have a headache."

Navy nodded, pressing her lips together so she wouldn't cry. She was shook up, and she wanted nothing more than to return to her apartment and—

She cut off the thought, because she was hundreds of miles from Dallas and her comfortable apartment. No, the only place she had to go back to was a run-down shack with ice cold water shooting from the shower head.

"Which pharmacy?" the nurse asked, and Navy just shook her head.

"Send it to White's," the doctor said. "I'll go talk to Squire." He left, and the nurse finished.

"Come out when you're ready," she said before following the doctor and leaving Navy in the cold room alone.

She sat sandwiched between the two huge cowboys while they waited for her prescription. Rode between them as they rumbled back to the ranch.

And Squire kept his hand on her elbow as he guided her toward his homestead. "My wife made dinner. Come eat, Miss Navy."

"I'm not going to sue you," she said, flicking a glance at him and then Pete. "Or you."

Squire grinned, but it only stayed for a moment. "That's a relief. But really, we just want to make sure you're okay."

"You live alone, right?" Pete asked, pressing in very close to Navy as if she'd tumble right down the steps Squire was leading her up. "New in town?"

"I don't live here," Navy said. "I'm just renting a place for a few months." And yes, she lived alone. Wanted to be alone so desperately right now.

Squire opened the door and the most delicious scent of pot roast hit Navy, eradicating all thoughts of driving herself back to town without eating first.

Her stomach, traitor that it was, growled loudly, and a measure of relaxation melted through her.

Then gorgeous Gavin Redd entered the kitchen, and

Squire released her to give his wife a quick hug. "Oh, good, you made Gavin stay."

"He's not happy about it," Squire's wife muttered as Pete settled Navy at the bar.

"Why aren't you happy about it?" Squire turned to Gavin. "We can talk about the job."

Gavin's eyes flew to Navy's, and a hint of color entered his face. "I can come back when things aren't so crazy."

Squire laughed then, and his wife and Pete joined in too. "Go sit," his wife said. "This is as un-crazy as it gets around here."

So Gavin followed her directions and took a seat at the table. Pete nudged Navy over there too, and then he nodded to Squire and left through the sliding glass doors they'd come through.

"Where are the kids?" Squire asked.

"Chelsea came and got them."

"My sister," Squire said, taking a seat. "Oh, and Miss Navy, this is my wife, Kelly."

"Nice to meet you," Navy murmured, feeling very much like she was on a double date. She threw a glance at Gavin, but he was arranging his napkin on his lap like he was about to eat at the ritziest restaurant in town.

"So Navy," Kelly said, spreading her own napkin across her lap and removing the lid from a glass dish of mashed potatoes. "What brings you to town?"

Panic pranced through her, and she felt very much

like Charcoal must have earlier—like she wanted to bolt and run as far and as fast as her legs would take her.

"Oh, just needed a break from work."

Gavin seemed very interested in the conversation, at least until it turned to other things. He started speaking with Squire, while Kelly kept the chat with Navy alive single-handedly.

Finally, dinner ended, and Squire shook hands with Gavin. "You'll make sure she gets home okay?"

Gavin gave a curt nod and gestured for Navy to go first out the door and down the steps. At least he didn't steady her, though it she wanted a man to touch her, it would be him.

*Stop it*, she told herself. He'd spent the whole meal talking with Squire about a job at the ranch, and if there was one thing Navy now knew for certain, it was that she didn't want a ranch life.

But she couldn't pinpoint why not. Kelly was obviously content and happy. And Three Rivers Ranch had grown considerably since the last time Navy had been here. If they had a grocery store and a gas station, it could become it's own town.

Riding back into town with Gavin felt seven shades of awkward, and thankfully he kept the radio at a loud enough level so talking wasn't required.

He pulled onto her lane and went all the way down it, until the headlights shone against the front door, before he stopped.

"Thank you," she said, finally finding her voice. "For the ride. And for saving me on that horse." She turned toward him, her emotions rioting now. What if he hadn't been there? How much longer could she have held on?

"I can come by tomorrow about eight to look at the place," he said.

She nodded and got out of the truck before she did or said something she wouldn't be able to fix.

THE NEXT MORNING, Navy startled when a knock sounded on the door at the exact moment the clock flipped to eight. She shook her head, unsurprised of Gavin's prompt arrival. She'd been unable to find much to dislike about him—and she'd tried. But no one in this town had anything bad to say about him.

He went to church. Helped his grandparents. Even served as a volunteer firefighter and served pancakes during their annual Flag Day breakfast.

If anyone had wondered why Navy, a newcomer to Three Rivers, was asking all over about Gavin Redd, they hadn't said anything.

He knocked again, and Navy bolted toward the door. She practically ripped it off it's hinges in her haste to open it, and the stunning sight of Gavin's handsome face on the other side should be criminal.

"Hey," she said, leaning into the frame. It squeaked

loudly, and she cringed as she straightened. He wore a blue T-shirt with the outline of Texas on it and jeans, which wouldn't have sent her heart into palpitations if it wasn't for the sexy tool belt slung around his waist.

"Hey." He seemed distracted as he glanced at the roof, the doorway, and past her into the cottage. "How many nights have you been livin' here?"

"Just three." She eased back so he could enter. As he passed, the spicy, masculine scent of his cologne entered her nose. She took a deep breath and committed the smell to her memory. "There're a lot of problems."

He glanced at her, a twinkle in his eyes for only a moment before he scanned the room again. "I don't think this is fit for human habitation."

"I didn't pay hardly anything for it." She gathered her hair into a ponytail and secured it with the band around her wrist.

"How long are you going to be here?" He pulled a tape measure out of the tool belt he wore and fitted the end of it against the floor.

"Six months." She folded her arms and leaned her hip against the kitchen counter. "I took a leave of absence from my job in Dallas."

His gaze met hers again and something huge surged between them. She had no idea what it was; had never felt anything like it. Waves of desire pulsed through her. Desire to get closer to him. Desire to touch his hand. Desire to spend more time with him.

*Please let him take this job*, she thought. The Shepherd's had authorized her to hire someone to make the improvements. Gerry had said he could spare five thousand dollars. Not that Navy was going to be staying long-term, but she'd overheard Gerry and Olivia talking about making the cottage a permanent rental, and that was when she'd entered their kitchen and asked about the remodel. With her timing perfect, she'd gotten the money and approval she needed.

Gavin cleared his throat, which broke the spell between them. "So, uh, I'd fix up these walls. Repaint." He scuffed his cowboy boot against the kitchen linoleum where it stuck up. "Redo this floor and make it go all the way through the living room."

He stepped toward her as the dollar signs in her head exploded. "What did you do in Dallas?" He extended that tape measure again, jumping from one conversation topic to another in a single breath.

He really must not have been eavesdropping last night, as she'd told all of this to Kelly. "I'm a pediatric nurse."

His eyebrows went up. "Wow. Impressive."

"I love it," she said. "I do. It's just...." She trailed off, not quite sure how to express how she felt about her job. She *did* love it. But she also knew she didn't want to have her entire life be about a job she liked.

Her ache to be a mother hit her in the chest, made her

gasp. Gavin turned back to her, his dark eyes full of concern now. "You okay?"

She nodded, because she wasn't sure she could speak past the pinch in her throat.

"I'd replace the roof," he said, going back to the home improvements. "And you said something about a water heater?"

"It doesn't really work." Navy had opted not to shower that morning, because she wasn't sure she could stand the nearly cold spray on her back.

"Do you know where it is?"

She stepped between the dining table and the couch toward one of only two doors in the cottage. "There's an equipment room off the bathroom." She crowded into the small space, Gavin right behind her. Once inside, she sealed them in the bathroom together, her nerves firing things like *He's so close.*

*You could touch him now.*

*Breathe deeper!*

With a slight tremor in her hand, she twisted the knob of the door behind the bathroom door. "In here." With the door open, she stepped back, her calf hitting the toilet bowl, so he could see.

He somehow maneuvered his broad shoulders into the tiny space and peered inside. Only a moment passed before he said, "Oh, this definitely has to be replaced." He twisted and drank in the bathroom too. "This isn't too bad."

"I think the toilet leaks," Navy said.

He couldn't get to it with her in the way, but she couldn't get out with him blocking the door. A smile bloomed on her face. "Sorry, if you'll just—" She silenced as he put both his hands on her waist. She gazed up at him, completely mesmerized by this man. She really needed to know his astrological sign, stat. After all, if he wasn't an Aquarius, what would be the point of starting something with him?

*What's the point anyway?* she wondered, the moments between them lengthening. *He lives here. You don't.*

But she did for six months. Her smile turned somewhat wicked, and Gavin even returned it. "Ah-ha," she said. "You do smile."

He twisted her past his body so she stood by the door and he stood near the toilet. "Of course I smile. You think my face is broken?"

"I was starting to wonder." She leaned into the closed door. "Besides, Chip said you're real serious when on the job."

"Chip Goldbloom?" Gavin rolled his eyes now. "You shouldn't believe anything Chip tells you."

"No?" Navy's smile widened. "I liked him."

"When would you have even talked to him anyway? I didn't know the karaoke bar was open during the day."

"I ran into him at the grocery store. Apparently there's a big karaoke event tonight. *Huge.* We should go. I mean, after you tell me how much this is going to cost and I take a nap to rest my fractured hand."

He looked at her hand. "You have a fractured hand?"

She gave a light laugh. "I think I probably gripped the saddle horn too hard. Stupid, right?"

He gazed at her with something akin to pity on his face, something soft she really wanted to get lost in.

"It's not stupid. That horse was flying."

Navy didn't want to talk about it, relive it. She'd already tossed and turned most of the night, thinking she'd heard a horse nicker and then scream.

"So, karaoke tonight?"

"*We* are not going to karaoke night." Gavin got down on his knees and fiddled with the toilet handle before flushing it. Sure enough, the hint of water formed around the bottom of the toilet. "What else did you need me to look at?"

There was only one other room in the cottage: her bedroom. A stream of self-consciousness stole through her before she remembered nothing in the bedroom was hers. Nothing besides the clothes, at least.

She pressed back into him in order to open the door, but he didn't put his hands on her again. Slightly disappointed in that and his reaction to her suggestion that they go to karaoke night together, she moved quickly back into the main living area of the cottage and over to the second door.

"Walls and stuff in here," she said once in the

bedroom. "And I swear that curtain rod is going to fall in the night and impale me."

Gavin chuckled, which sent warmth through Navy. He'd seemed so stoic in the few times they'd been together. Almost angry with her. Probably because of the birdhouse comments.

"I can fix that," he said, moving back into the living room.

"Okay," Navy said. "Honesty up front. I have a limited budget. The water heater has to be done. Does the roof?"

"If you want to stay dry." He pointed to a discoloration on the linoleum. "That's from leakage when it rains."

"But we're headed into summer, so in the next six months, is the roof necessary?"

"Well, *I* think a roof is necessary."

"Well, I have five thousand dollars."

He sank onto the couch. "That does change things." He took out a stubby pencil and a notebook the size of his palm and started writing. He muttered to himself, glanced up at the ceiling a few times, and then ripped off the page.

"For five thousand dollars, I can do it all except the roof."

"What can you do with the water heater and the roof?" It wasn't her cottage. The Shepherd's could pony up more money to fix the roof. She'd lived in Texas her whole life, and she knew it hardly ever rained in the summer.

"The water heater, the roof, and that curtain rod."

"Everything but the roof then." Navy extended her hand for him to shake, and he got to his feet.

He studied her fingers for a moment and then put his in hers. A zing shot up her arm and down her ribs, and a spontaneous smile spread her lips.

"Deal," he said, pumping her hand.

"When do I pay you?"

"When the job's done."

"How long will that be?"

"Three weeks." He looked thoughtful for a moment. "Unless I get that job at Three Rivers."

She wanted to ask him all about that, but she decided she didn't have to do it right now. "Do I need to be home?"

"Why? You have big plans for while you're here in Three Rivers?"

"Yes," she shot back. "I'm planning to read a book a day, soak in the sun, and maybe do a little touring around this historic town."

Gavin laughed, the sound fun and filling the cottage in only a moment. Navy tried not to bask in the tonalities of his voice, let them infect her, but it was entirely impossible. Gavin Redd possessed some serious Southern charm, and she had no defense against it.

"We really should go to karaoke night," she said when he'd quieted.

"I believe you promised me dinner. But I don't sing." He inched closer to her.

"How about breakfast?"

His gaze turned into a glare again, but it softened after only a few seconds. "Sure, breakfast. But no karaoke."

She giggled and resisted the urge to slip her hand into the crook of his elbow. "You're no fun."

"I'm a lot of fun." He followed her outside. "Want me to drive?"

She waited until he'd closed the door before asking, "So what's your story?"

"My story?"

"Yeah, why are you here? How long are you going to be here?" She watched him find something else to look at. Watched that strong jaw tighten and release.

Navy sensed a really juicy story. She tipped forward onto her toes because she didn't want to miss a single word.

# Chapter Six

Gavin couldn't ignore the chemistry between him and Navy. He wanted to, if only to protect himself. For all he knew, Grandmother had matched them and he simply didn't know it yet. Good thing was, Navy didn't either. That, or she showed an incredible amount of restraint.

Grandmother didn't normally match women with a specific man anyway. No, Navy had probably gotten some advice about where to hang out to meet her match. Or what cologne to watch for. Or even something like a star sign or a birthstone.

"I was born in Amarillo," he started. "My aunt still lives there, but my parents are in West Virginia now."

"Siblings?"

"No."

"Intriguing."

He wasn't sure why being an only child mattered at all—unless it was something Grandmother had told her to watch for. He suddenly didn't want to share anything about himself with her.

"And now I live here to help my grandparents. They're getting older." He nonchalantly waved one hand and pulled it off pretty well. "I mow the yard and fix up things around the house. That kind of stuff."

A hundred yards passed under the truck's tires before she said, "That's it?"

"I'm pretty boring."

"You are not," she said. "There's more, and you're just not telling me."

Gavin's teeth worked against themselves. "What did my grandmother tell you?"

"I—well—"

"See, I've been approached by her clients before, and well, I'm not interested in that. To be blunt."

Navy sputtered for a moment. "That *was* blunt."

"And I've dated a few blondes too," he said. "Didn't end well for me. I'm thinking I need a brunette. No offense."

"No offense?" Navy sounded incredulous. "Well, then, none taken." But she clenched those arms tighter around her body and stared out her window.

Minutes passed while he navigated the roads down by the Bark Park. He cast a look at the dogs running in the morning light and realized it had been too long since he'd brought Blue to his favorite patch of earth: the dog park on the outskirts of Three Rivers.

He would tomorrow, after church. He cast Navy a glance as she watched the landscape pass. "Do you have dogs?"

"Three," he said. "Well, really only one. The other two are my grandparents', but they've sort of adopted me as their dad."

"I had a cat in Dallas."

He detected the note of sadness in her voice. "What happened to her?"

"I had to give her to my aunt so I could come here. But my aunt loves cats, and she really wanted me to come, so it's okay." She tucked her hands in the back pockets of her jeans. "She was matched here, you know. Fifty years ago."

"Grandmother did it then," Gavin said. "She just celebrated her fifty-second anniversary as Three Rivers's matchmaker."

"I know. My aunt told me all about her."

Gavin wasn't sure where this conversation was going and if he'd like it. He glanced way down the block to where the karaoke bar sat, and he turned away from it. Anything was better than that. He didn't want to tell Navy that he actually sang just fine. He just didn't do it in public after the Debbie Debacle.

The karaoke bar wasn't even open in the morning, thank goodness. He parked in the lot at the pancake house, which was packed with Saturday morning customers, and got out of the truck. "Did your aunt find her match?"

"Yep. She and Uncle Marvin have been married for forty-nine years."

He froze, his heart rat-a-tatting in his chest. "Uncle Marvin?"

*Forty-nine years* screamed through his mind.

"Not only that, but Aunt Izzie found Uncle Marvin the very next day after your grandmother's matchmaking reading. The very next day!" Navy sounded absolutely delighted and hadn't seemed to notice that Gavin's muscles had seized.

Navy was the niece Izzie was always mentioning. His "Aunt Izzie" and "Uncle Marvin" were her blood relatives?

What were the chances of that?

Gavin didn't know, but the scientist in him told him that it was probably a really minuscule percentage. The romantic side of him whispered that maybe he and Navy were meant to be. The realist wanted more time to explore, to hold the woman's hand, to maybe see if a beautiful blonde woman wouldn't chew him up and spit him out.

"Marvin worked at Three Rivers and then Sterling Silver Ranch," Gavin said, his voice tinny. "When it was still a working ranch. They live somewhere in Hill Country now."

Navy froze too. "Wimberley. How do you know that?" Her lovely eyes widened and searched his.

"I stay with them every year when I go do auctions down there." He took at step, but Navy didn't. "I need to call them, in fact. Make sure I can stay this year too."

Navy caught up to him. "But she's not your aunt."

"No, but I call her that. She's my grandmother's best friend."

"She *is* my aunt." Navy's voice sounded strangled, alien. "She's the reason I came to Three Rivers."

Gavin couldn't believe that, if only because it made things a lot more complicated than they needed to be. He didn't believe in magic, or myths, or matchmaking. He barely believed in coincidences. He shook his head. "You came to Three Rivers because you work a demanding job and needed a break." He'd heard her say that last night, whether he wanted her to know he'd listened to almost everything she'd told Kelly.

"I came to see your grandmother."

Gavin's jaw hardened. He really wished Navy would've come for another reason. *Any* other reason. "Whatever," he said, pulling open the door to the pancake house. "Let's take our food over to the park. You want to?" He didn't want to eat under the scrutiny of the townspeople for a second time. Thankfully, Navy agreed, but a wall of applause hit them the moment they stepped into the pancake house.

There was no way he was escaping with a to-go box of blueberry pancakes now.

"There he is!" someone yelled, and an older gentleman clapped Gavin on the shoulder.

"You're a hero, son," he said.

Gavin looked at Archie Combs blankly. A hero?

"And look! He's with the woman he saved."

Gavin switched his attention to Navy, who looked just as baffled as he did. She smiled like a champion though, her expression turning wise and wonderful at the same time.

"Let's go," he muttered, slipping his hand through her elbow. Despite the dozens of eyes from seemingly everyone in town, he still felt a massive jolt of attraction move through him at the physical contact with Navy.

But she wouldn't go with him. "Oh, come on, Gavin," she said, laughing. "You better enjoy these fifteen minutes of fame."

But Gavin didn't want to enjoy even sixty seconds of it. Wished he could be that horse and gallop away from this place. Instead, he pasted a smile on his face and started shaking hands with the townspeople of Three Rivers like he'd singlehandedly solved the world's energy crisis.

And hey, he got a free breakfast for jumping off a fence and onto a moving horse. So that was something.

*  *  *

Gavin's mind didn't stop turning until he slid onto the bench beside Grandmother the following morning. The sunlight streamed through the stained glass window in front of him, and he closed his eyes against the blue and purple light that bathed this section of the chapel.

And just like that, his mind started up again. He'd barely slept. Barely been able to brew a pot of edible coffee. Barely been able to do more than the involuntary bodily functions.

All because of Navy.

She was like a parasite, taking his systems down fast.

He'd wanted to call Aunt Izzie and ask about her niece. He dismissed that as too obvious, and besides, he enjoyed the weeks and months it took to get to know a woman. At the same time, his brain urged him to go a little faster this time, because Navy wasn't going to be in town for very long.

*Then he'd think, Six months is a long time. She's been here for three days, and you've seen her each of those.*

"Can I sit with you?"

He glanced up to see none other than the very woman who'd been plaguing him. Navy batted her dark eyelashes and put that gorgeous smile on her face. Did she know she could charm armies with that smile?

Something told Gavin that no, she didn't. She probably knew she was pretty, but she had no idea the havoc she was wreaking on his pulse, his stomach, his muscles, his brain, his very life.

"Scoot down, Gavin," Grandmother said, probably not for the first time judging by the slightly acidic bite in her tone.

Gavin scooted. Gavin started straight ahead. Gavin wanted to bolt, because church was his escape. It was where he came to reset himself for the week. To renew his faith. To reevaluate what he should be doing with his life.

"Glad I made it on time," Navy said a bit breathlessly. "I couldn't find anyone who knew for sure if the time was ten or eleven."

"Pastor Adams changed it to eleven a year ago," Gavin said woodenly. "Gets more people here if it's a bit later." He personally didn't understand that, but he also rose at the crack of dawn. The dogs needed to be taken out, lawns needed to be mowed before the heat of the day, nails needed to be hammered before housewives grew cranky. And hopefully, if Squire would ever call him, ranch work would need to be done before the heat of the day settled over Texas.

"Now I know."

The presence of Navy next to him was anything but soothing. She smelled like flowers and soap and something more sensual that Gavin couldn't name. She wore her nails short and her hair in loose curls around her face and a dress the color of plum skins. With a broad white stripe near the hem, which just reached to her knees.

She was the picture of beauty, and Gavin wanted to slip his hand into hers. He'd touched her before—the bathroom episode played through his mind during the opening hymn. He couldn't concentrate on anything the preacher said. He thought that if he could just hold Navy's hand, everything inside him would finally settle.

So he reached over and folded his hand over hers. His fingers slipped between her thumb and fingers, and he simply rested his hand on top of hers.

She startled a little and turned her face to his. All his bravery had been used on getting his hand across the six inches between them, so he couldn't look at her.

Pastor Adams's words became audible. With every moment that she didn't pull her hand away, Gavin's pulse steadied. After about thirty seconds of the awkward hand position, she turned her hand and their fingers found their way between each other. Naturally. Easily. Like her fingers belonged in the empty spaces between his.

A smile crossed his face against his will. He wasn't sure what he was trying to hide, and he slid his eyes toward her without moving his head.

She was smiling too.

# Chapter Seven

Navy didn't hear a word the pastor said after Gavin claimed her hand. Oh, no. She spent the next hour obsessing over her choice to accept his fingers into hers.

When they stood to sing the closing hymn, she clasped her hands in front of her and mouthed the words. Gavin next to her belted out the lyrics in a rich baritone that gave away his singing ability.

"You do too sing," she hissed as they sat down for the closing prayer.

"I *can*," he whispered back. "Obviously. But I *don't* sing."

"You mean in public."

"Shh."

She bristled. He'd just shushed her. *Shushed* her! Sure, okay, an elderly woman had just started the prayer, but really?

She leapt to her feet before the final "Amen," finished and made it to the back of the chapel before most patrons had even stood. She escaped the church with its quaint red brick and charming stained glass window. She'd had no idea if Gavin attended this church or not, but she couldn't say she was disappointed. Seeing his charcoal-colored cowboy hat had actually made her heart thump in anticipation.

And then he'd held her hand. She wandered over to a large bur oak and leaned against the trunk. *At least you know the feelings between you go both ways,* she thought. He'd been a mystery since the moment she'd met him, and she smiled. She liked mysterious men.

*In Dallas, she told herself firmly. You like mysterious men who live in Dallas.*

She twirled the banded silver ring on her thumb. Around and around it went, in time with her spiraling thoughts.

*You're a nurse. You can work anywhere.*

*But I live in Dallas. My family is there.*

*You left for six months.*

*But I like my job in Dallas.*

Around and around, until Gavin said, "Hey, there."

She turned toward him, her panic doubling when she felt something crawling on her arm. She yelped and brushed at the huge black bug.

Gavin stood as still as a statue, his face unchanging.

"What was that?" She examined the ground for the horrible insect.

"You don't have bugs in Dallas?"

"Of course we do."

"Maybe you should get back inside and start praying to rid Texas of nasty animals."

She cocked her head, trying to read his mind. Of course she couldn't, but she did deduce that he really liked teasing her.

"Earth would be improved without snakes," she said, playing along with him. "I don't know what the Good Lord was thinking by putting them here with us."

But if there were no snakes, would her horse have spooked? Would Gavin have saved her? Maybe snakes weren't as bad as she'd originally thought.

Gavin's tough guy façade broke, and he grinned at her. "Navy." He ducked his head, and she found his shyness adorable. When he looked at her again, redness resided in his cheeks, and she liked that too.

"Do you want to come to the bark park with me and my dogs?"

"When?"

"Right now. I mean, this afternoon." He shrugged, exhaled, and glanced away. "I'm forty years old. You think I'd be better at this."

*You're more suited to a mature man.*

Nancy-the-Matchmaker's words appeared in her mind. "You're forty?" she asked.

He stroked his beard. "My gray hair didn't give it away?"

She shook her head as a thrill the size of a yacht went through her. "My dad went gray when he was about thirty."

"Hmm." Gavin extended his hand toward her and said, "Want me to drive?"

"I don't actually own a car," she said. "Well, I do. But I left it in Dallas."

"Let me guess. You took the bus up here."

"It's part of the legend."

"I'm aware."

Navy let her feelings radiate with a bit of hurt for a few steps. "You do realize I'm not whoever broke your heart, right?"

His cowboy boots stuttered against the concrete. "I never said—"

"You didn't need to." Navy gave him what she hoped was a reassuring smile. "Sure, I'm blonde, and yes, I rode into town on a bus. Maybe I even believe what your grandmother told me. Doesn't mean I'm going to hurt you."

"Women like you have."

"You barely know me." She started to withdraw her hand from his, but he gripped the ends of her fingers.

"I know," he said. "I'm...sorry."

That was all. Nothing more. No excuses. No further explanations either. Just an apology. While Navy would've appreciated another installment of his obviously bumpy past, she appreciated the simplicity of how he communicated.

"So there are three dogs," he said as he opened the passenger door for her. "Blue is a yellow Lab."

Navy giggled and tucked her skirt under her legs. "How did that happen?"

"I adopted him from the pet shelter, and the first day I brought him home, he dipped himself in some blue paint I was using for a sign."

"Cute."

He closed the door and walked around the front of the truck. As he went, his lips moved, like he was muttering instructions to himself. Navy couldn't help laughing, couldn't help the rush of warmth that poured through her, couldn't help but think that maybe she *had* come to Three Rivers to find a groom.

* * *

Forty-five minutes later, she'd changed into a pair of shorts and a tank top the color of lemons. He'd put on a pair of basketball shorts and a T-shirt with a bull on the front and the words "Eight second loser." He'd left the cowboy boots somewhere in his house and traded them for a pair of flip flops.

He'd disappeared around the side of the house and three dogs had preceded him back to the front yard, where she waited in the truck. She grinned at the happy look on the yellow Lab's face.

A giant black dog followed him, and a shorter, blonde pug after that. Gavin pointed to the truck and barked a command she couldn't hear. All three dogs obeyed, and the truck vibrated and rumbled as they jumped in the bed.

"What kind is that black one?" she asked when he got in.

"A Newfoundland. My granddad loves them."

"He's huge."

"He'll last about five minutes at the bark park," Gavin said, setting a backpack between them on the bench seat. "But I brought treats and water, and he'll just lay in the shade until Blue wears himself out."

Navy had never been to a dog park, and she worried the amethyst on her middle fingers.

"You wear a lot of rings," he said.

She glanced at her hands, where she wore a ring on every finger on her left hand and three on her right hand. "I suppose I do."

"Do they mean something?"

"This one does," she said, admiring the amethyst. "I bought it for myself after my boyfriend proposed to my sister."

The beat of silence that followed screamed through the cab. "Wow," Gavin said. "I think that's—well, you've got me beat."

Navy laughed, though the sound did still carry a few

notes of disappointment. Maybe hurt. Maybe embarrassment. She wasn't sure.

"I thought he was going to propose to me. He took me to this fancy restaurant downtown." She did a half an eye roll. "Okay, semi-fancy. I thought that was it. We'd been dating for just over a year. Instead of breaking out a ring, he broke up with me. Told me he was in love with my little sister, Lexie." She exhaled, realizing her chest hadn't collapsed once. She hadn't felt like crying while speaking. "They were married six months later, and they have a baby now."

"I'm so sorry."

"Most days I think I'm over it." The first clip of uncertainty cut through her. "Then sometimes I feel like the whole situation is so unfair. So I don't know."

"Life is unfair," he murmured. "Just like Pastor Adams was saying today. It's not fair, but through Jesus Christ, we can be assured that we will get our reward."

Navy nodded and gave him a close-mouthed smile, as she hadn't actually heard the pastor say that.

"I want to buy my own ranch," Gavin said. "That's one of my unfulfilled dreams."

"So you're not a carpenter?"

"I am, I guess." He pulled into the parking lot but didn't kill the engine. "It's what I do right now to get by. But I'm a cowboy, through and through. I worked at Sterling Springs Ranch before they converted to a wedding venue. I was the foreman at the B&B before they nearly went bankrupt. I have a degree in ranch management. I'm hoping to get a job at Three Rivers real soon, and I want a ranch of my own."

"Cattle ranch?"

"Yeah. Acres and acres of land. And cows. And chickens." His expression grew distant, and Navy envisioned him on a ranch, running it, riding a horse with the wind trying to steal his hat. It was a beautiful picture and fit him like a glove.

"You'll get your ranch," she said with confidence. She lifted her chin and smiled. "Now, let's go see these dogs in action." She got out of the truck and met Gavin at the tailgate. All three dogs sat, waiting for him to give them the command to get out.

"There's one ball," he said, pulling it from the backpack. Blue's tail went *whap! whap! whap!* against the metal. "Blue, let Misfit get it sometimes, okay?"

"Misfit?" Navy laughed. "Which one of you is Misfit?"

"The pug."

"Oh, you're not a misfit." She spoke in a cooing voice she usually reserved for newborns and scratched the dog's ears.

"There's a Great Dane here," Gavin continued. "Miles, no...funny business. I will leash you." He backed up a step but put his hand up, palm toward the dogs. "Ready? All right. Go."

The dogs leapt from the truck as a unit and tore past a

few cars to the green space. Blue barked once and sprinted like he'd been caged for days.

"Jeez, Gavin. Do you ever let them out?"

"They roam the yard," he said. "They just act like they never get any exercise." He joined the dogs on the grass and threw the ball. Blue and Misfit tore after it, but Miles didn't seem to notice or care. He sniffed another dog half his size, his tail wagging wagging wagging.

Navy watched Gavin throw the ball over and over for Blue. Misfit never did get it, and eventually she gave up. Miles had flopped within five minutes, as Gavin had predicted. But Navy enjoyed the sun on her bare arms and legs. Loved the country breeze against her face. Admitted that she really liked the company she was with.

Gavin asked, "Hey, you wanna go to Tampa this weekend? They have a pretty great Hodgepodge Market my grandmother likes to visit."

Navy had noticed Gavin always called his grandma "grandmother." She wondered about that as well, wondered when Gavin would open up to her beyond that he'd been hurt by a blonde woman in the past.

"What's a hodgepodge market?"

"It's row after row of booths. Homemade items. Antiques. Refurbished stuff. They have it twice a year, and it's fun."

"You like to go?"

"I like that Grandmother buys lunch and entertains

me with stories on the way." He shrugged with a smile. "I figured you might like it too."

Navy would. But she also wanted to know what this was. A date? A Saturday outing with his grandmother? Was she a tagalong? Or had he invited her purposefully?

She wasn't brave enough to ask. But she did like spending time with Gavin, so it wasn't too terribly hard to say, "Sure. Pampa this weekend."

# Chapter Eight

Though Gavin wanted to rush the several blocks south and then east to Navy's cottage at first light on Monday morning, he didn't. He puttered around the house with a cup of coffee in one hand and a pen jotting notes for her home improvement in the other.

Then he went next door to see what Grandmother had prepared for breakfast. She didn't cook a full breakfast every morning, but on Mondays she usually did because she always had leftovers from Sunday dinner. And they'd had steak last night.

So Gavin was hoping for some steak and eggs that morning. He wasn't disappointed, and he pressed a kiss to his grandmother's forehead when she looked up from the pan where the delicious smell of meat and cheese and eggs emanated. "Morning, Grandmother."

"Hey, sweetheart. Will you go check on your grand-dad? He's not up yet, and that's a little strange."

"Sure thing." Gavin moved through the kitchen and down the hall. Granddad hadn't been getting up as early as he used to for about a year. The strength in his dominant hand had worsened considerably, and he'd confided in Gavin that most of his fingers usually tingled as his carpel tunnel syndrome affected him.

Granddad had been a master cabinet maker. Gavin had learned all his woodworking skills from him, something for which he felt a wash of gratitude.

"Granddad?" Gavin eased open the door with two fingers and peeked inside. The bed was empty, but Gavin couldn't see anyone anywhere. He went back down the hall, even sticking his head into the bathroom to make sure his granddad wasn't in there.

"He's not there," Gavin said, his concern starting to rise.

"What?" Grandmother didn't look up from the eggs.

"Granddad's not in bed," Gavin said slowly, warning in every syllable.

That got Grandmother's attention. "What do you mean?"

"I mean, he's not in bed. He's not in the bathroom either." He glanced over his shoulder, past the table and chairs to the vacant living room. "I don't know where he is."

Grandmother put down her wooden spoon. "He must

be outside with the dogs." But the tone of her voice suggested her own worry.

"I'll find him." Gavin pushed down his hat and exited the house from the same door where he'd entered. He scanned the road in front of the house. No traffic. No people. Nothing.

"Blue!" Gavin called, adding a hearty whistle to his call. The dog barked, the sound distant and behind the house. Gavin turned that way, hoping Blue would lead the pack and Granddad would bring up the rear.

His stomach growled as all three dogs came into view. "Let's go!" he called, waiting until little Misfit arrived, her tongue hanging out of her mouth. "Where's Granddad?" He looked across the green expanse. Couldn't see anyone.

He lifted his right fist. "Blue. Sit." He gave the dog a few seconds to settle and listen. "Find Granddad." He kept his fist up and Blue trembled, waiting in anticipation. "Find Granddad." He popped his fingers open and Blue took off.

Gavin followed, almost jogging after the Labrador retriever. The other two dogs yipped and wove across the lawn also, and Blue rounded the smokehouse in the back. He barked. Barked again. Finally Gavin got there, and Blue took off across the street toward the Old Main Hill Bed & Breakfast that sat defunct and took up several blocks. The For Sale sign swung in the breeze, and Gavin's boots hit the asphalt at the same time Blue started barking like he'd been set on fast-forward.

Relief cascaded through Gavin, because the barking meant Blue had found Granddad. Around the broken down well and toward a cabin, he finally spotted his granddad sitting on a ratty-looking bench on the front porch.

Blue shuffled forward and back, left and right, barking his fool head off. Gavin approached and said, "Blue. Got him," and the dog quieted and settled onto his haunches. Gavin examined his granddad, who wore his usual baggy blue jeans and a collared plaid shirt. This one was red and the sleeves looked well worn near his elbows. "You okay, Granddad?"

"Just fine." The older man looked up at Gavin, kindness in his blue eyes.

"What are you doin' out here?"

"I went for a walk."

Gavin sat on the bench next to his granddad, hoping the structure would support his weight. It creaked and groaned and Gavin prepared himself to hit the dirt. He hoped he could catch Granddad before a hip fracture. When the seat shifted, Gavin shot to his feet.

"Did you get lost, Granddad?" Gavin asked in the gentlest voice he could conjure.

"No, no." He shook his head and stroked Blue's head. The panting of three dogs mixed with the shallow breeze. "I just got tired. Decided to rest."

"What hurts?"

"Nothing." Granddad stood on somewhat rickety legs,

but Gavin didn't reach for him. He didn't want his granddad to feel weak, or old, or like he needed help. Still, his muscles tensed, ready to assist if necessary. "I just got tired."

"How long were you walking?" Gavin stepped when Granddad did, and it took an excruciatingly long time for a few feet to be covered.

"An hour or so."

"You didn't tell Grandmother? She was worried about you."

"She wasn't awake yet."

How she'd thought Granddad was still in the bed when she'd gotten up, Gavin wasn't sure. He wasn't sure who he should be worried about: her or his eighty-five-year-old grandfather. Probably both.

"Well, she has breakfast ready." They made it across the property and stepped onto the road. Grandmother came out of her matchmaking door, her hand fluttering around her throat. Gavin increased his pace and intercepted her. "He just went for a walk and got tired. He's fine." He moved out of the way and let his grandparents have their conversation. Gavin watched them for a moment, watched the way Grandmother's hands lilted on Granddad's arms and shoulders, just to be sure he really was fine. Watched as he kissed her cheek and reassured her he was fine. Watched as their love became evident for all to see.

He turned away, his throat thick. He wanted that kind

of love in his life. And not with a yellow Labrador retriever, though Blue licked his fingers and a surge of affection for the dog dove through him.

* * *

Gavin never made it to breakfast, which was a real shame. But he did deliver his granddad back to the house before his phone rang.

He practically tripped as he tried to walk and answer it at the same time, his heart hammering with anticipation.

"Hey, Squire," he said.

"Gavin, how are you surviving?"

He glanced over his shoulder, half-expecting someone to be standing there watching. So many people watching since they'd heard about his "heroic" rescue out at the ranch. "Just fine," he said.

"I'm hopin' you're in a position to move out to Three Rivers and join us."

"I am," Gavin said, his mind flowing in about a dozen different directions. He hadn't mentioned the job at the ranch to Grandmother, nor had he arranged for anyone to check on them.

He also had the job at Navy's to do, and the drive into town and back would take an insane amount of time.

"Great," Squire said. "How soon do you think you can make it?"

"I can start work whenever you say," he said. "I need a

couple of weeks, maybe three, to get things squared away with my grandparents." That would give him time to finish the job at Navy's too.

He wanted the job out at Three Rivers Ranch. He did. But the idea of owning and operating his own ranch still swirled within him, and Navy's declaration that he'd have it one day seemed to grow louder and louder by the moment.

"Take the time you need. I'm doin' some repairs on the cabin where you'll live. Or rather, I'm about to ask you to do the repairs on the cabin where you'll live." He chuckled. "In addition to that, I want you to work in the office, like we talked about."

"Ranch management, right." He had a degree on the topic, after all.

"You can ride too." Squire wore a smile in his voice. "I know you love your horses."

Gavin couldn't deny it and he laughed. "I sure do. But maybe not that wild one from the other day."

That got Squire to laugh too, and the call ended soon after that, with Gavin agreeing to come out to the ranch and get started the next morning.

He turned his face toward the sky and whispered, "Thank you," into the open blueness above him. Then he faced his grandparent's house and tried to find a solution for them.

Nothing came to mind, so he held onto his news, intending to tell them once he had an idea for who come take his place as their gardener, caretaker, and dog-watcher.

* * *

AN HOUR LATER, properly fed and with a gallon of ice water in a cooler at his feet, he raised his hand to knock on Navy's front door. He hit it twice.

It fell into the cottage with a deafening *bang!*

Navy screamed and when the dust cleared, Gavin got an eyeful of her standing there with a chimney poker in her hand.

"It's me," he said, stepping over the door and into the cottage. "Don't start stabbing."

"Gavin." Her chest heaved as she breathed in and out several times. "What are you doing?"

"I knocked. That door needs to be replaced." He gave it the evil eye. "Obviously."

"You don't know your own strength." She put the poker back in the basket next to the fireplace and gave him a flirty smile.

Gavin examined the hinges while his face heated. "These are rusted through." He sighed. "I guess I need to get to the hardware store first. You'll need a door to hold in the air conditioning."

"I'll come with you."

He scanned her, taking his sweet time as he drank in her cutoffs, strappy sandals, chilled iced tea on the end table, and a shirt the color of poppies. Her blonde hair looked almost white against the red, and her blue eyes completed the patriotic look. He'd always been extremely devoted to his country, and he licked his lips as his eyes traveled back to hers.

She wore a knowing glint in her expression. "What? You think I can't handle the hardware store?"

"Your shoes are lacking," he said.

She laughed, a girly little sound he liked. "My shoes are fine. Let's go." Navy marched right over the fallen door and onto the patch of grass that grew right up to the house. Gavin didn't have much choice but to follow. She gathered her waves of golden hair as she neared his truck and wrapped an elastic around her ponytail. She slid all the way over on the bench seat so that by the time Gavin climbed into the cab, her thigh was flush against his.

"So I looked up a few festivals going on around here," she said. "And I found this one called Women Gone Wild."

"Oh, boy," Gavin said, a chuckle immediately following his words.

"It's a really great thing. Really." She shoved his arm when he kept laughing. "Listen to this. 'Just for women. Just for fun.'" She read from her phone. "Kayaking, archery, fly fishing, team events, arts and crafts, and more." She looked up at him. "I totally want to do that."

"You like kayaking and archery?" Gavin would have to rethink everything he'd assumed about her if she said yes.

"I've never done either."

As he'd suspected. "Where is it?"

"Vincentville. Where's that?"

"Oh, let's see." He blew out his breath. "At least a three-hour drive." He cut her a glance out of the side of his eye. "And you don't have a car."

"We could maybe go together."

"Just for women," he teased. "Just for fun. I'm not getting anywhere near that."

"Stop it." But she joined in his laughter and leaned her head against his arm until they arrived at the hardware store.

"What other festivals did you see?" he asked as he put his hand on a flatbed cart and pulled it into the hardware store.

"Tons," she said. "Music stuff, and art shows, and there's so much to do during summertime in Amarillo, which is only an hour away."

"It's a pretty great place."

"Will you buy a ranch near here?"

Gavin's breath hitched, and he thought of the job at Three Rivers Ranch, and then his grandparents. "I'd like to, yes."

"Have you found anything?"

"Nothing I can afford," he said. "And honestly, I haven't looked in a while."

She danced in front of him. "Why not?"

"I've been busy." He focused on the shelves above her

head, though he didn't need anything automotive to fix up Navy's cottage. "Let's go look at paint, all right?" Maybe with her absorbed in the trillions of shades of gray, she wouldn't ask him any more questions about the dreams he had but had neglected.

# Chapter Nine

Navy woke on Saturday morning, a feeling of euphoria coursing through her she didn't recognize. In fact, she hardly recognized her life at all. She'd spent a week's worth of evenings with Gavin in her house, as he'd gotten a job as a bonafide cowboy out at Three Rivers Ranch. He left early in the morning and came by her place about four-thirty each afternoon.

If he was suffering from all the extra work and lack of sleep, he didn't say anything. Didn't look like it either, as he always had a smile for her. Things in the cottage were coming along just fine. He had all the ceilings painted and the walls prepped. He'd fixed that curtain rod the very first day, and the hot water heater had been installed on the second, so Navy's life had improved dramatically already.

She'd been sleeping better than ever. Waking with a smile on her face. She had read a book a day and soaked up the sun while she waited for Gavin to come over. Then she spent her time perched on a narrow piece of furniture while she watched him work. They'd talked about his childhood and hers. She'd told him about her time in nursing school and about every story she could think of about the newborns she cared for. He'd detailed a little bit more about the kind of ranch he wanted, and he'd spoken about his grandparents in a loving voice.

He'd told her about most of the people in town, but what she really wanted to know—his romantic past—he had remained tight-lipped about. Extremely tight-lipped.

And she didn't want to ask. She looked at herself in the mirror. "Do not ask him. He'll tell you when he's ready."

She wished there was a myth or a ritual she could do to get a man to spill his secrets, but the only idea she had was to get a fistful of pennies and find the nearest fountain, throwing them all into the water as she made her wish.

She let the idea move back and forth, front to back, as she braided her hair. She put on a flirty sundress in purples and blues and pinks and slipped on her strappy sandals that made Gavin roll his eyes. But she was pretty sure this type of footwear was acceptable at a hodgepodge market. A hodgepodge market that they were attending with two people over the age of eighty.

She slicked on her favorite pink lip gloss and grabbed her purse. She wandered down the dirt tire tracks toward the street, where Gavin would see her when he arrived. Before she could get there, his truck turned onto the lane, and she moved to the grass to wait for him.

He got down out of the truck and for a moment, Navy thought he'd sweep her off her feet and then plant a kiss on her lips. The disappointment when he didn't was severe and swift, and it was then that Navy realized how deep she'd already fallen.

"Morning," he said instead. "It's a tight fit, but I think we'll make it. It's only an hour to Pampa."

She peered past him and into the cab, where Nancy watched her with an extreme look of interest. Navy put on a smile that felt timid and tired, and allowed Gavin to help her into the truck. She glanced at the tiny patch of space behind the steering wheel. No way Gavin would fit there. Maybe one of his legs.

He somehow managed to squish himself onto the remaining seat, and he leaned into her to slam the door. "Oof," he said before twisting so most of his weight rested on the door instead of her.

An awkwardness filled the cab that Navy didn't know how to crack. But Nancy said, "Gavin said the work at your cottage is coming along nicely."

"It is," Navy said. "Having hot water was such a huge improvement, I'm not sure anything else is needed."

"Oh yeah?" Gavin asked. "You think not having a front door is okay?"

"Well, *someone* knocked it down." She grinned at

him and glanced at Nancy. Her smile faded at the placid look on the elderly woman's face. "He knocked it down."

"It was an accident, Grandmother," Gavin said over Navy's head. "The hinges were rusted through."

The conversation flowed easily to Aunt Izzie and Uncle Marvin, and Navy was just beginning to enjoy herself, cramped as she was, when Nancy asked, "So how have things been going on the match-front?"

Navy froze, and next to her, Gavin stiffened. She didn't dare look at him. Her voice cracked when she said, "Oh, I'm not looking, Nancy. Remember? I'm on my escape from reality right now."

Nancy patted her knee. "Oh, that's right. Must've been the other girl who said she was staying right here in Three Rivers until she found her match."

Navy swallowed, but her mouth tasted sour. Her stomach squirmed. "How many women do you help each week?" she asked.

Gavin cleared his throat, but Navy still didn't look at him. It was an innocent question. The matchmaker could choose to answer or not.

"It depends," she said. "But heading into summer, we'll get a lot more. I had four last week."

"Sometimes she has two or three each day," Matthew, Gavin's granddad, said, his first contribution to the conversation at all.

"Wow. Two or three a day." Navy let the topic drop,

and Gavin picked it up with, "Granddad, how's Aunt Ally doing?"

Navy let the conversation about Gavin's aunt continue without her. Her mind marinated over what she'd said, and how Gavin would perceive it, and what she could do to fix the damage before their relationship was deemed terminal.

As soon as they arrived at the hodgepodge market, she excused herself. "I just need to make a quick phone call." She flashed what she hoped was a winning smile and scampered away.

"Please don't be working today," she muttered as she pulled up Lynn's phone number and hit call. "*Please* don't be working today."

The phone rang once, twice, three times. Navy's hopes crashed, then soared when Lynn said, "Girl! You finally called."

"Hey, Lynn." The relief swept through her so quickly she couldn't keep it from infusing her voice.

"What's going on? Did you meet a man already? You've been up there what? A week?"

Navy bit her bottom lip, her emotions spiraling all over the place. She pictured her best friend with her dark hair and light eyes. She had soft hands and quick wit and had taught Navy to always watch for the tiniest of details when it came to babies. Lynn was married, with two teenagers, and by all accounts, she and Navy shouldn't be so close. But they were.

"You better start talking," Lynn said. "Or I'll send Roy up there to find out what's going on. Or he'll just put out a call. I'm sure the Sheriff in Three Rivers knows you're in town and can go check on you."

"Don't send your cop husband here," Navy said with a light laugh. Lynn was forever threatening to sic Roy on Navy. "But I did meet someone."

A squeal nearly deafened Navy. "Shh," she said. "It's not what you think."

"What I think is you got on a bus and went five hundred miles north to find your match. And you met a man."

She hadn't figured out a way to ask about his birthday yet. And though Nancy had said a few other things, none of them really defined Gavin as her match. "He's a great guy. Handy with a hammer. Tall. Handsome. A cowboy."

"Sounds dreadful."

Navy giggled again, glancing over her shoulder to see where Gavin and his grandparents had gone. They were moving down the row of parked cars at a snail's pace. She followed at a distance so that she wouldn't be overheard.

"But I wasn't—I mean, what if there's a guy in Dallas I'm supposed to meet? I was only here for vacation."

"Just trust the process," Lynn said.

But Navy didn't know what that meant, or how to trust something she didn't understand. Her own process of trying to find a boyfriend had never worked, and as far as she could tell, she wasn't doing anything different with Gavin.

"I don't know the process."

"You know," Lynn said. "Dating, going out, spending time together. See if you like him."

Oh, Navy liked Gavin. She knew how to flirt with him. How to get him to look at her with that flame of desire in his eyes. How to make him laugh. Since she'd dated so much, she knew exactly what to do.

And that was exactly the problem. She was still doing what she'd always done. So she couldn't expect a different result this time.

Gavin glanced over his shoulder, prompting Navy to say, "I have to go, Lynn. I'll call you later."

"You better. I want more regular updates now that I know there's a man in play."

Navy smiled, hung up, and hurried to catch up to Gavin. She let her fingers brush his, but he didn't grab on. She didn't either. It was obvious he didn't want to flaunt their budding relationship in front of the most famous matchmaker in Texas.

Navy supposed she couldn't blame him for that, but a terrible thought struck her right between the ribs. Maybe he'd brought her out here so no one else in town would find out about their hand-holding.

She tried to dismiss the thought. They'd gone to The Stable together. The bark park. The hardware store.

Still, the idea wouldn't go away. Gavin had never

openly displayed his affections for her, limited as they were. Only when they were alone.

*That's normal, she told herself. This is new.*

She closed her eyes as Gavin stepped up to the ticket booth and said, "Four, please."

She prayed that she wouldn't ruin this thing with Gavin—whatever it was—before it could truly get started.

# Chapter Ten

Gavin enjoyed wandering around the hodgepodge market with Navy and his grandparents. They ate too much fried food from a truck, laughed, and told stories. He liked Navy's quick smile, her helpful hand when Granddad stumbled, her calm demeanor in tough situations. He chalked all of those admirable qualities up to her pediatric nursing training.

*But he couldn't get her words from that morning out of his head. Oh, I'm not looking, Nancy. Remember? I'm on my escape from reality right now.*

Her escape from reality. So holding his hand wasn't real for her? Or the way she watched him with those penetrating eyes, practically begging him to come over and kiss her? That wasn't real?

He hardened his resolve, pushed out the disruptive

thoughts. He wasn't going to be her vacation boyfriend. This wasn't a fling for him.

So he couldn't hold her hand again. It wouldn't kill him. He'd learned that a broken heart didn't actually kill a man when Joan had left him standing out at Sterling Springs Ranch by himself, at a wedding altar he'd constructed with his own hands.

A jilted groom, right there in Three Rivers, Texas, which was famous all over the state for its matchmaker. No wonder he disliked the town's history so much—and every woman who rolled into town on a bus and went straight to his grandmother's door. And Navy fit right into that group as if she were their founder. So had Joan.

He sighed, alerting Blue to his mental and emotional turmoil, as he kicked off his boots and leaned back into the couch. He'd dropped Navy off thirty minutes ago and made sure his grandparents were safely inside their house after that.

For Saturday night, it was early still, but Gavin's exhaustion nearly overwhelmed him. His phone chimed, and his heart shot to the back of his throat. Maybe it was Navy.

It wasn't. Instead, Steve's name came up on the screen. "Hey," Gavin said, his troubles evaporating. "How was the trip to California?"

"Good," Steve said. "Great. You should come next time."

*Right*, Gavin thought with an eye roll tacked on. "I

don't want to infringe on your family vacation," he said in the nicest voice he could muster.

"Carol wouldn't mind."

"I'm sure she would." Gavin cleared his throat. "So what's up?"

"Wondered if you wanted to go fishing tomorrow after church."

"Yeah, sure." It was a ninety-minute drive to the Kingsland Slab where they fished, but Gavin suddenly craved the time away from Three Rivers, away from Navy, away from everything that had become normal in his life. Squire had given him this first weekend off, promising there wouldn't be many more once he moved out to the ranch.

"Anything new happen while I was gone?" Steve asked, as if he'd already heard. Since his wife was a waitress at the speciality coffee shop, one of the premier hotspots for talk in town, he probably had.

"Got a new job fixing up the Shepherd cottage," he said. "Got a new job at Three Rivers. That's about it."

"Right," Steve said. "So you didn't save a blonde woman and then start dating her?"

Gavin made a choking noise. "Is that what people are saying?"

"You're a big topic right now, what with the way you leaped off that fence." He chuckled, which only riled Gavin further. "I wasn't even there, and I seem to know every detail."

"It wasn't that big of a deal," Gavin said, wondering how many times he'd have to say it tomorrow. Fishing and a long drive suddenly didn't seem so fun.

"And you didn't go out with her?"

"I mean, we got breakfast, but only because she's new to town and the cottage where she lives is barely habitable." But it was more than that, and Gavin knew it. But maybe for Navy, their pancakes-in-the-park had been part of her vacation.

"Okay, well, I'll see you tomorrow then."

Gavin hung up, knowing full well he'd have to tell Steve everything. Gavin had a few friends in town, but not many. Most knew what had happened with Joan and had let him retreat to his quaint house, the dogs, and his grandparents' massive yard. Steve had been there the longest—since Gavin's days at Sterling Springs Ranch even.

Gratitude filled him that he had someone rational to talk to about his maybe-relationship with Navy. He couldn't mention anything to Grandmother, not after the Joan disaster. After all, she'd consulted with Joan four times over the course of a year before she accepted his proposal. And four months later, she skipped town after yet another meeting with his grandmother.

Gavin had never asked her what she'd said to Joan. He wasn't sure he cared, because he thought it was all bunk anyway. The legends and myths. The matchmaking. All of it, pure fantasy.

Which meant Navy—and any hope of having a real relationship with her—was pure fantasy too.

GAVIN MADE sure to sit on the inside of his grandparents the next day. He wasn't trying to be rude. He simply needed to protect himself from the blonde bombshell who walked in with sixty seconds to spare, her hair all twisted up like she was going to the prom and a dress as dark as night clinging to her curves.

He sucked in a breath as she sat next to Grandmother, as they started whispering, as she glanced down the row to him. He gave her a single nod and focused on the pulpit, every cell in his body angry at him for not sitting where he could touch Navy.

Pastor Adams spoke about enduring through trials, and Gavin kept all his attention on the man's words. Gavin had been through a fair few trials, from losing his job to all the dating fiascos. His grandparents were aging, and he expected he'd lose one of them in the near future.

His unfulfilled dreams of owning a ranch came forward in his mind. He hadn't been looking, and something whispered to him that he should be. *But what about the new job at Three Rivers?* he thought.

*And just after that, What am I going to do with Grand-mother and Granddad?*

And he wasn't sure where the next thought—*Call Aunt Ally*—came from, only that it was there.

His spirits buoyed, and a new plan fell into place to start the search for a ranch again and to call his aunt about moving to Three Rivers to help with her parents. He'd mentioned it to her a few times before, but she'd been reluctant to leave her job in Amarillo. Gavin understood, but more time had passed, and perhaps she could retire or find something to do in Three Rivers—or move her parents closer to her.

The service ended, and Navy appeared at Gavin's side. "What are you doing this afternoon?"

"Goin' fishing with a friend."

Her eyebrows rose and her eyes widened. "Oh. I didn't know you liked to fish."

"It's Texas," he said as if that explained everything.

She fell a half-step behind, and Gavin felt bad for dismissing her so readily. "Have you ever been to the Canadian River? It's gorgeous."

"No," she said. "I did see it a lot on that website I was looking at about the festivals."

"Yeah, they do stuff all summer long. The fishing is good about now until June. Steve and I will go a lot."

Steve stepped in front of them as if summoned by the mention of his name. "Gavin." They man-hugged, complete with loud clapping on their shoulders. "And you must be Navy Richards."

A pit opened in Gavin's stomach. If Steve knew that,

he already knew everything else. Sure enough, he kept his winning smile in place for Navy as he shook her hand, but his eyes flashed to Gavin's several times.

Gavin settled his weight on his back foot and folded his arms. "So you'll drive?" he finally asked so Steve would stop talking to Navy.

"Yeah, I'll be there in say, forty-five minutes?"

"I'll be ready." Gavin tipped his hat to Navy and walked out of the church. He hoped she'd follow, that maybe he could stop by her place tonight to show her his catch, but he made it to his truck without her.

His phone remained silent while he put together his fishing gear, food for the afternoon, and an assortment of toys for Blue. Misfit and Miles wouldn't come—Gavin didn't trust them in the Canadian River in the spring.

Steve arrived, and Gavin hefted his gear and backpack into the truck bed. "Thanks for embarrassing me at church," he said.

Steve, a ginger-haired man who couldn't grow a beard to save his life, laughed. And laughed. "She's nice."

Gavin grunted, put up the tailgate, and got in the truck. Steve joined him, still smiling. "And beautiful."

"She came to Three Rivers on a bus and met with my grandmother the very next morning."

Steve cringed as he backed onto the street and set the truck heading east. "I can see why you like her, and why you don't."

"She'll only be here for a few more months." *At least*

*five more*, he thought but kept to himself. "And I'm looking for a ranch, so maybe I'll leave town before she does."

"Anything good out there?" Steve asked. He'd taken to equipment repair, a service offered by the hardware store, when most of the ranches around town had dried up.

"Maybe," Gavin said. "I haven't looked in a while, but I feel like I need to again."

"I'll come work for you."

"I know you will." The conversation turned to Steve's vacation, and how Gavin's parents were doing in West Virginia, before circling back to Navy.

"She's from Dallas," Gavin said. He filled Steve in on everything he knew about Navy, which was admittedly a lot more than he'd told her about himself.

"So does she know how you feel about the legends of Three Rivers?"

"I think I've been clear."

"But she doesn't know about Debbie. Or Ginny. Or Tabitha. Or—"

"No," Gavin barked to get him to stop talking about all his past female failures. "She doesn't know anything about any of them."

"It's nothing to be ashamed of."

"Says the man who married the woman who came into town on a bus and met my grandmother the next morning."

"It was two mornings later," Steve said with a smile.

His grin faded quickly. "But seriously, Gavin, sometimes it does work out."

"Sure." But Gavin had five examples of how sometimes it didn't work out. And he wasn't up for a sixth.

Thankfully, once they started fishing, the conversation stalled. Gavin soaked up the warmth of the late-April sun. Snacked on his beef jerky and homemade trail mix that Grandmother put almond M&Ms in. Cast his line over and over, hoping for that bass to latch on.

The beauty of Texas surrounded him, and he let the gurgling sound of the river soothe his soul. Allowed the clean breeze to sweep the cobwebs from his mind. The gray and brown rocks, the bright green grasses and trees, the brilliant blue sky all combined to create a picture of perfection Gavin was sure didn't exist anywhere else on God's great earth.

And he was thankful God had put him here. Right there in Texas, where he could experience a slower pace of life. He felt closer to the Lord while fishing than he did while sitting in church, and Gavin finally cast all his burdens away while he cast his line out again and again.

Several hours later, he said, "Thanks," to Steve as they pulled up to Gavin's house. "We should go again next weekend."

"Let me check with Carol."

Gavin collected his gear from the back of the truck, waved to Steve as he drove off, and had taken two steps toward his front door when Navy came around the side of the house, both Misfit and Miles panting at her side.

# Chapter Eleven

Navy could see and sense the wall Gavin had constructed between them. She'd dated enough men to know, talked to parents who were resisting treatment, had a sixth sense about such things.

So she was sure he'd put his defenses in place. What she wasn't sure of was *why*.

"How was the fishing?" she asked.

He lifted a lidded basket. "Great. Here's dinner." He watched her with amusement, like she'd balk at eating bass.

"Great," she said without batting an eyelash.

Gavin stepped to his front door and entered the house. Navy had not gone inside earlier, but she did now. The inside of Gavin's house was neater than she'd thought in some ways, and messier in others. There were no dirty dishes in the kitchen, but the living room held discarded socks and unfolded blankets, almost like he slept on the couch most nights after kicking off his cowboy boots.

"Give me a few minutes." He moved down a hall, adding, "Make yourself at home." A door closed a moment later, and Navy took the opportunity to snoop. Problem was, Gavin didn't have a whole lot for her to draw from. There were two pictures in the front common area of the house. One of him and his grandparents, obviously taken a few years ago as his beard didn't hold any of the gray streaks it did now. And a photo of him and who she assumed were his parents. His father had the same sloped nose, the same twinkling, mischievous look in his eyes when he smiled.

Dust didn't cover anything, which meant Gavin did a fair bit of cleaning, and Navy couldn't smell anything foul. He didn't return right away, so Navy sat on his couch. Almost immediately, Blue jumped up next to her and put his paws—his damp and dirty paws—in her lap. Right on her khaki shorts.

"Blue," she said, leaping to her feet. "You're dirty." She swiped at the mud smeared on her clothes.

Gavin chose that moment to return, his cowboy hat gone and his hair damp. He wore his basketball shorts and a gray T-shirt. He paused on his way into the kitchen and looked at her. Navy froze, unable to even continue cleaning herself. Experiencing him in his natural environment, shoeless, hatless, and his stunning physique, and Navy couldn't move. Could barely breathe.

"Let's go, Blue," Gavin said and the dog trotted over to him. He opened a door next to the garbage can in the kitchen and Blue went through it. "You guys too." Misfit and Miles, who hadn't done anything, followed and Gavin closed the door.

He scanned her again, making her blood heat. He'd looked at her in this way several times now, and every time felt like the first time. "Let me get you a washcloth." He moved into the kitchen and started rummaging around in cupboards and drawers.

He finally faced her again. "It looks like I don't have a washcloth. Grandmother will, though."

"You don't cook," she said, the pieces of his flawlessly clean kitchen coming together.

"Nope." He grinned at her. "So let's get these fish next door so Grandmother can put lemons or something on them." He picked up the basket and stepped toward the door. "What are you doing here?"

"I wanted to talk to you." She didn't want to tell him she didn't have any other friends in town besides him. Surely he already knew that.

Gavin didn't ask what she wanted to talk about or continue the conversation. He took Navy next door and said, "I have six bass here, Grandmother."

She bustled out of the kitchen, wiping her hands on her apron. "Wonderful, wonderful." She took the basket and disappeared back the way she'd come.

"We're gonna go for a walk," Gavin called. He didn't

wait for an answer before heading outside again. He took several long strides away from the road and into the back-yard before asking, "So what did you want to talk about?"

"Yesterday," she said. "I had a good time."

"Me too."

"Did you?" She tilted her head and looked at him. He'd stuffed his hands in his pockets, the exact opposite of what she wanted him to do with them.

"Sure," he said. "Did you see that new lampshade? I put it on the lamp in the living room."

"I must've missed it." Had she misread the signals from him too? She inched a bit closer to him on her next step, and he remade the distance between them when he stepped. Nope.

She stopped walked and drew in a deep breath. "It seems like you're unhappy with me."

Gavin stilled too. "Not at all."

Navy examined him, trying to see past the symmet-rical face, the sexy salt and pepper hair, the impressive muscles. "Did I do something yesterday?"

He gazed back at her evenly. "Not at all."

"What did I say to upset you?"

He blinked twice in rapid succession. Ah-ha. So that was it. She'd said something. Her brain whirred and stirred, trying to find what it could've been.

"Nothing."

She bumped him with her hip and started walking again. "You're such a liar."

"Navy—"

She froze again, all this stop and go making her stomach lurch. "It was the thing about me looking for a match." She peered at him, getting that tiny flinch again. "Isn't it?"

His eyes transformed as she watched, from displaying his agony, to his anxiety, to his anger. "I don't believe in the stupid legends."

"Your opinion on that has been made very clear." Navy's defenses flew into place now too. She worked to put them down so she could really listen to him.

"I'm not interested in dating another woman who's seen my grandmother."

"Were we dating?"

His eyes stormed with aggravation, and he started walking again. "Seriously, Navy. I'm not interested." But everything about his voice and his stature screamed that he was lying.

"Yes, you are." She hurried after him and put her hand on his arm to get him to stop. He did, and she slid her fingers down his forearm to his hand, where she linked hers with his. "I can tell that you are."

"So what?" he asked. "I'm not your match, which means you'll leave town as soon as you figure that out. *I'm not interested* in chipping off another piece of my heart for another pretty woman." He ground his teeth together. "I'm really not."

"How do you know I'm not your match?"

"Experience." He folded his arms.

Navy wanted to reach up and erase the pain from his expression. "What did they do to you?" she whispered. He was so good, so gentle. How could anyone not see that?

"Let's see," he said with a long sigh. "Debbie wanted to know if I could sing. So I sang for her. But see, I wasn't the right height. *The right height.* So that ended pretty quick. And there was this one woman named Tabitha. Things were going great with her until Grandmother told her she needed someone born in nineteen-seventy-five. So that was me. Because you know, a couple's entire compatibility depends on *what year they were born.*" Every letter dripped with sarcasm and scorn and sadness.

He scoffed, the sound full of bitterness. "And the real kicker—the last woman I dated for two years left me standing at the altar by myself while she hopped on the bus and rode out of town." He glared at her, and glared hard. "So you'll excuse me if I'm not a fan of that blasted myth and everyone who believes in the fantasy of it."

Navy had no idea what to say. She'd wanted—craved— this part of Gavin's story. She'd just had no idea it would be so tragic, or so opposite of how she felt about the legends of this town.

He muttered something under his breath, but Navy couldn't decipher it. Her mind spun with information, with emotion, with indecision. She'd been flirting with him for a solid ten days. But if she found out he wasn't an Aquarius, would she abandon him?

She really wanted to say *No, of course not*. But the truth was, her heart started a war with her brain.

"So what do you need to know?" he asked.

"I-I d-don't know," she stammered.

"Sure you do." He looked at her angrily. "My grandmother told you something. And it wasn't that your match lived across the street from her."

Navy opened her mouth, determined to make something up. Instead, she said, "She said my best match would be an Aquarius. Because I'm a Libra."

Gavin's fury came immediately, almost a scent on the air. "Great." He stomped back toward his house. "I have no idea what that means."

"It has to do with your birthday," she called.

"February seventeenth," he said, his long strides putting so much distance between them so fast.

Numb, Navy sat in the grass and pulled out her phone. She looked up the dates for the Aquarius zodiac sign, and sucked in a breath. January 20 to February 18.

She jumped to her feet and searched the horizon for Gavin.

Gavin, who *was* an Aquarius.

* * *

Later that night, Navy sat in the backyard with her laptop balanced on her lap. She'd searched for "cattle ranches for sale in Texas" and nearly closed the computer from the sheer volume of listings that came up. No wonder Gavin was overwhelmed and had stopped looking.

She narrowed her search to the panhandle area, and the choices went down. The prices sure didn't though.

She clicked and frowned. Read listing after listing. Navigated to a new real estate website that included all commercial properties and performed the search.

A bed and breakfast came up, and she straightened. The Old Main Hill B&B looked charming and like the heart of Texas. And it sat right across the street from Gavin's house right here in Three Rivers—and certainly didn't look like the pictures online.

But it could be perfect for Gavin. Navy copied the website and sent it to herself so she could text it to Gavin. She hesitated, not wanting to be the first to make contact since their mini-argument that afternoon. It was one of her dating tactics—make the man initiate contact after a confrontation.

*I want a different result*, she thought. The breeze whispered to her that she needed to do something different.

So she wrote up a text about the B&B and put the link at the end. She hit send before she could second-guess herself. Her second text said: *Oh, and you are an Aquarius, in case you were wondering. Do you have time for lunch tomorrow?*

# Chapter Twelve

Gavin ignored his phone the four times it chimed. His embarrassment wouldn't fade, and he didn't want to interact with anyone until he felt more human. His stomach growled with want of those bass he'd caught, but he didn't want to face Grandmother without Navy at his side. She'd ask a zillion questions about where Navy had gone, and why hadn't Navy stayed for dinner, and when was Gavin going to call Navy again.

He sighed and stared at the flickering TV as darkness fell. He woke when his phone rang, and he fumbled along the top of the couch until his fingers touched the plastic case. He squinted at the bright light and hit as close to the green circle as he could estimate. Thankfully, the call picked up. "Hello?"

"Gavin, it's Granddad," Grandmother said.

He was instantly awake and throwing his legs over the

side of the couch. "Granddad?" He reached for his boots. "Talk to me, Grandmother."

"He woke up, complaining of pain in his stomach."

"Maybe it was something he ate."

"He started coughing, and there's blood."

Gavin stood. "I'm on my way over. Call the ambulance." He hung up and pulled open the front door at the same time. He jogged across the street by the light of the moon. The front door banged against the wall, and Grandmother obviously hadn't made it out of her bedroom to turn on any lights.

He hit his leg against the chair and groaned. After making it to the kitchen, he flipped all the switches he could find and headed down the hall. Granddad sat up in bed, a washcloth in one hand and a miserable look on his face.

"Did you call the ambulance?" he asked Grandmother, who stood near the bathroom with the phone hanging at her side.

"They're coming," she whispered, her voice feeble and tired.

"All right." Gavin scooped Granddad into his arms. "I'll wait with him in the front room. Get dressed, Grandmother. We'll follow the ambulance."

"I want to ride with him," she said stronger now.

"You still need to get dressed." Gavin gave her a quick smile and went down the hall. He didn't like how little Granddad weighed in his arms. "How are you feeling?"

"I feel like I need to throw up," he said. "But I can't."

"When did you start coughing?"

"Oh, I've been coughing for weeks now."

Gavin didn't like the sound of that, or the hint of pain in his granddad's voice. He put him on the couch and sat beside him. "Any blood any of the other times?"

"No." Granddad looked at the washcloth like it could diagnose him. "I'm old, Gavin."

"We'll get you fixed right up." Gavin spoke with confidence he didn't feel. He sat with his grandparents for the few minutes they waited for the ambulance to arrive. With both of them loaded in the back of the bus, Gavin headed across the street and climbed in his truck.

He exhaled and ran his hand through his hair. It was two-thirty in the morning, but he felt wide awake, ready for anything.

*Well, maybe not anything*, he thought as he swiped on his phone and saw that he'd received two text messages from Navy. Two from Steve as well. He opened those first, and found one about the fishing trip and one about next week's fishing trip. The normalcy of the messages calmed Gavin further.

*He read Navy's two messages, the last one burning his retinas. Oh, and you are an Aquarius, in case you were wondering. Do you have time for lunch tomorrow?*

He didn't care about what astrological sign, or zodiac sign, or whatever an Aquarius was. But for some strange reason, he did want to have lunch with her tomorrow.

He looked up and out the windshield at the stars hovering above him in the sky. He wasn't sure what would be going on with Granddad tomorrow, so he couldn't commit to Navy. Not to mention that he couldn't make a ninety-minute round-trip from the ranch, where he now had a job.

The job at Three Rivers.

It was everything he'd wanted for months, but now, it seemed to complicate everything. He quickly swiped and tapped, hoping Squire slept with his phone on silent.

*My granddad is ill. I won't be able to come out tomorrow. Hope that's okay.* He read over the text a second time and sent it flying across cyberspace.

He didn't want to text Navy right now. So he set a reminder for himself so he wouldn't forget to let her know he couldn't make lunch.

Her first text required more thought, more time. A bed and breakfast? His eyes narrowed at the link. His thumb waited over it. He didn't tap, didn't want to think about taking on a bed and breakfast when his lifelong dream had been a cattle ranch.

"How are those two things even close to the same?" he wondered to himself. His voice cut the silence around him, and he put the phone down on the seat. He drove toward downtown, catching the ambulance pretty easily, his mind churning over the thought of managing cabins full of bed and breakfast patrons instead of cabins full of cowboys.

* * *

Hours later, he still didn't know why Granddad had been coughing up blood. Grandmother slept in the recliner in his room, leaving Gavin to the uncomfortable waiting room chairs, the giant saltwater fish tank, and the low drone of *The People's Court* on the television nearby.

He'd texted Navy by eight o'clock, but she'd just answered with, *Oh, no. I hope your granddad is okay. Keep me posted.*

And *No worries about lunch. I'll go with Jana.*

*Jana who?* he typed out and sent.

*Jana Cheeks. Do you know her?*

"I know everyone in Three Rivers," he muttered. "Especially the women." He didn't put that in his text, though. He just said, *Yeah*, and let it go. People like Navy didn't understand how small towns worked. She'd never lived in one, so he couldn't expect her to, but still. She should know about the town gossips, the best place to get burgers in the middle of the afternoon, and how if you waited until Saturday night at the bakery, you'd get the cupcakes for half-price because they weren't open on Sunday and couldn't hold their stock.

And Jana Cheeks was the town gossip. How she'd latched on to Navy was a mystery, though she did spend all day here in town while he went out to the ranch.

But maybe he'd missed her going into the hair salon. He thought about his obsession with her blonde hair, and

112

he didn't think so. He yawned and decided to leave the Jana issue alone for now. Navy was a smart woman; she'd figure things out.

*She's making friends*, his mind whispered as he slouched down far enough for his head to rest on the back of the chair. *That's not what someone does when they're just in town for a few months.*

The more irrational side of his brain wanted to argue back, but he was too tired. It seemed like only minutes later that Grandmother came out, pushing Granddad in a wheelchair. Gavin jumped to his feet and went to take over the manual labor from her.

"What's goin' on?" he asked. "Why didn't someone come get me?"

"His chest x-ray was clear," a doctor said. She had a warm smile and a baby duck attached to her collar. "He has a mild case of bronchitis, which we've treated with antibiotics here and your grandmother has a prescription for more. We believe he ate something bad last night, and he had some acid reflux at night, which caused the lining of his throat to be tender. So when he coughed from the bronchitis, there was some tearing and thus the bleeding."

Gavin could hardly absorb so many words at once. "So he's okay?"

The doctor smiled, and Gavin wondered if Navy looked as comfortable when she dealt with anxiety-ridden patients. "He's okay, Gavin." She put her hand on his bicep. "Go home and get some sleep." She looked at Grandmother and Granddad. "All of you."

"Thanks." Gavin nodded and pushed Granddad toward the exit with Grandmother shuffling along beside them. By the time Gavin got everyone taken care of: Granddad with his antibiotic and soda water, Grandmother with a plate of scrambled eggs and toast, and all three dogs with their food and water, Gavin wanted nothing more than to sleep.

He set an alarm for midday so he could still go get something done at Navy's, and collapsed into bed.

*Thank you for helping my grandparents*, he thought just before drifting off to sleep.

He dreamt of a place he didn't recognize. A lot of tall buildings, and hundreds of cars, and many thousands of people. The city reminded him of Austin, but it wasn't Austin. Or Dallas. But it was definitely Texas.

He walked down the street and met Aunt Ally at the end of the block. She spoke, but the words were silent in the dream. She handed Gavin a key, smiled, and turned to leave. She got in the car with Grandmother and Granddad, and Gavin realized that she was taking them home with her.

He woke to his alarm, the remnants of his dream still wafting around inside his mind. He picked up his phone and silenced it, then called his aunt.

"Gavin, dear, how is Granddad?"

"He's okay," Gavin said. "Sorry, I forgot to call. They

said he has a bit of bronchitis. So they're treating that with antibiotics. And they said he probably ate something bad, had acid reflux, so his throat was tender, and when he coughed, there was blood."

"So nothing serious."

"Nothing serious." Gavin rested his elbows on his knees. "Aunt Ally, have you thought any more about moving home to take care of them?"

He closed his eyes, a prayer beginning in his heart. He loved his grandparents. He did. But he'd been looking after them for a decade, and he was ready to start his own life.

"I met with my boss this past Friday," Aunt Ally said. "I'm putting in my retirement papers, and I'll be home by Halloween."

*Home by Halloween* sounded like music to Gavin's ears. "Great," he said, the word heavy with relief. "Thanks, Aunt Ally."

"Have you been looking for a ranch?" she asked.

Gavin thought of the B&B Navy had linked him to. He hadn't had the inclination to look at it yet. "Sort of," he said.

"You deserve a big ol' ranch with tons of cows," Aunt Ally said. "I know you'll get it."

"Maybe," Gavin said. He made small talk for a few more minutes before hanging up. Before showering and getting properly dressed. Before heading over to Navy's cottage.

His stomach rioted like he'd swallowed fire ants as he approached the front door. He knocked, but she didn't answer. He entered her unlocked house and found it empty. Her purse was gone, and he remembered she was going to lunch with Jana today.

That suited him just fine, and he pulled out the roll of plastic and began taping it to the floors and covering the furniture. Working felt good, pulled his muscles, made him focus on more than just himself. At the same time, he had a distinct feeling that God wanted him to focus on himself for just a few minutes.

*Where should I be? Gavin prayed as he worked. Here? Three Rivers Ranch? Somewhere else? Help me find the ranch where I should be.*

He didn't mention the B&B to the Lord, because Gavin didn't want to run a hotel that served pancakes and coffee. He couldn't even *make* pancakes, for crying out loud. But he could repair walls and tape baseboards and slather a new color inside a house, so he lost himself to the rhythmic tasks of painting.

# Chapter Thirteen

Navy sat across the diner table from Jana, a fellow blonde. "Thanks for meeting me," she said as the waitress handed her a menu. Navy flashed the woman a grin before realizing the plastic was a bit sticky. She made a face but hid it quickly.

"What can I get y'all to drink?" Lola-the-waitress asked.

"Sweet tea," Navy said, and Jana ordered the same.

Lola had barely walked away when Jana leaned into the table and said, "So what's going on with you and Gavin Redd?"

Navy hadn't even opened her mouth to answer before Jana continued. "All the girls at the salon are in a twitter. I guess a couple of them have been circling Gavin for a while, and he's so aloof. Does he act like that with you? I bet he doesn't. You're so pretty, and I bet he just talks your ear off." She giggled while Navy blinked, trying to process everything Jana had said.

"Anyway, Amy was saying she went out with him once a few years ago, and he was just so sad, you know?" Jana flipped her hair over her shoulder like she knew the inner workings of Gavin's soul. "I guess his girlfriend had just broken up with him. And before that, one of his girlfriends left town with another man. Darrel or Derek or somebody with a D-name."

Lola returned with their drinks, and Navy practically lunged for hers. Perhaps this lunch with Jana had been a bad idea. She'd gone into the salon last week to see if they carried any purple shampoo, as she enhanced her blonde hair with a brightening toner. Jana had helped her, and talked to her, and though Navy had friends back in Dallas, she didn't have any here.

So when Jana said they should go to lunch sometime, and Gavin couldn't go today, Navy had texted Jana. As the stylist talked, and talked, and talked, Navy regretted her decision. Thankfully, Jana moved past Gavin at the same rate she spoke, which only had one speed: fast.

Navy heard about the owner of Beaned, the specialty coffee shop down the street. The florist who'd been engaged twice and couldn't seem to get anyone all the way to the altar. Who had what dogs, and who let them run wild, and who'd switched to cats.

She'd never eaten so fast. A twinge of guilt pulled through her when her phone chimed and she seized onto an excuse that wasn't entirely true. "I'm sorry. It's my mother." It wasn't, and Navy kept the phone tilted away from Jana, who was looking. The woman didn't miss much, Navy would give her that much credit. "Thanks for meeting me for lunch." Navy smiled as widely as she could and slid out of the booth.

She paid while examining her phone as if she'd just received Very Bad News and left without glancing at Jana. She sighed as she ducked around the side of the diner and pressed her back into the gray brick.

The text wasn't from her mother. Or Gavin. But Lynn back in Dallas. *How are things in Three Rivers? We miss you here!* She'd sent a picture of the pediatric nurses pulling faces, and Navy's chest hitched.

She thumbed out a generic message about how everything was great and how much she missed her friends.

At least she didn't have to lie about that. She hadn't even been in Three Rivers for two weeks yet, and the sudden urge to return to her hometown and get back to work felt strange. Maybe she'd made a mistake by planning to stay for so long.

Then an image of Gavin's handsome face filled her mind, and she thought, *You'll probably need* longer *than six months to crack him.*

He *was* a bit aloof, but Navy had read up on Aquarius's, and they often were, especially at the beginning of relationships. So she'd determined that she simply had to be persistent. Not let him walk away from her with statements like, "I'm not interested."

She wandered around the bark park before heading over to a huge fountain and statue. Several tourists lingered in the same space, reading the historical markers and taking pictures. Navy did too, as if she didn't know about the myths of the matchmaker who lived here.

Her heart squeezed when she thought of the women who'd hurt Gavin. She understood why he didn't like the legends, but she couldn't simply rid herself of her fantasies either. For so long, she'd listened to the romantic stories Aunt Izzie told, saw how much she and Uncle Marvin loved each other.

She trailed her fingers along the bottom of the statue, the desire to have that kind of love with someone as strong as ever. So what if she'd believed in a silly tradition? She'd tried everything else, and Nancy had only helped her hone her focus from one type of man to another.

A more mature man, which admittedly Navy hadn't naturally looked for. Someone willing to listen to her, which most Aquarius men were really good at. That was when Nancy had said, "You should be looking for an Aquarius," and continued with why such a man would fit with Navy's personality.

As if a light from heaven had beamed straight onto her, a realization hit Navy. Nancy's words were advice, not law. She'd told Navy about *herself*, and what kind of man would mesh with *her* the best.

The matchmaking reading wasn't about who Navy's match was. It was a resource for knowing herself and then using that information to find a more compatible date—one that could turn into a husband.

She started laughing, and she snorted the way she did when she really got going. She was usually embarrassed by that; didn't let herself laugh full-out for fear the men she dated would find her snorting unattractive. The tourists looked at her, but she just kept laughing.

"I've got to go talk to Gavin," she said to the statue of the woman, who just kept gazing out at the prairie. Navy would not be this nameless woman—she would go to Gavin and see if he would listen to her.

But first, she fished a quarter from her purse and tossed it into the fountain with the thought, *I wish to sort through things with Gavin Redd.*

* * *

By the time she returned home, she was equally frustrated and relieved. She entered the cottage to find Gavin wearing a mask and wielding a long roller as he swept gray paint onto her walls.

"You are a hard man to find," she said. She went to set her purse on the table, only to see that he'd covered everything. The fridge, the stove, all the furniture. It was all taped under a layer of plastic.

He paused and turned toward her. He didn't wear his

cowboy hat, and she could only see his eyes, but still her heartbeat pulsed through her body. She wanted to talk to him, hold his hand, walk with him, maybe even kiss him. Today.

"And you have paint on your face," she said with a smile. She glanced around. "This looks like a war zone."

"I'm painting," he said through the mask.

"When can you take a break?"

He tilted his head slightly, a confused look in those gorgeous eyes. "A break?"

Foolishness raced through Navy. Of course the Man of Iron, Gavin Redd, didn't take breaks. "I'll be reading out back," she said. She stepped back out of the cottage, half-hoping he'd call for her to stay with him the way she had last week. He didn't, and she didn't want to throw herself at him. Besides, there was nowhere for her to sit and talk to him anyway.

Only ten minutes later, Gavin came around the back of the house, maskless and without the drips of paint on his forehead. He'd pushed his cowboy hat back into place, and he sat in the other chair at the table in the shade.

"You took a break?" Navy didn't look fully at him.

"You seemed like you wanted me to."

Navy put her e-reader down. "Let's go for a walk." She stood up, but he didn't.

"It's the middle of the afternoon," he said. "It's hot."

"You sound tired."

"I am tired."

"How's your granddad?"

"He's okay." He told her about a mild case of bronchitis and some acid reflux, and he didn't seem too concerned.

Navy reached across the table and covered his hands with hers anyway. Mostly because she wanted to touch him, see if that flame still roared between them. "I'm sorry."

He looked up and their gazes locked. The fire and desire between them was definitely still there, and very very hot. Navy smiled. "I like you, Gavin Redd."

He got to his feet, tugging on her hand to come with him. "Let's go for a walk."

Heat dove through Navy, and it wasn't all from the Texas sun when they stepped out of the shade. "I just want to say a few things," she said.

"All right."

She launched into what had brought her to Three Rivers, why she felt the magic of this place, why she'd thought seeing a matchmaker would help her. "I've just dated so much," she said. "I don't even think you know how much."

"How much?" he asked.

She let their hands swing between them for a couple of steps. "I quit dating two weeks before I came here. But the week before that, I went out with five different guys on five different nights. It was getting to the point of one-and-done. I couldn't find *anyone*."

Navy exhaled, her memories of those winter months in Dallas, meeting a man for coffee, or rushing home from the hospital so she could shower before a man picked her up for dinner. She even went straight from work to a breakfast date several times when she worked the night shift.

"And Aunt Izzie had told me all about Three Rivers, how much she loved this town, all about your grandmother. And it felt right." Navy shrugged one shoulder. "It felt right to come here."

He squeezed her hand. "Thanks for telling me all that." Gavin took a deep breath. "Are you planning on goin' out with a new man every night while you're here?"

Navy slowed her steps and stopped. She turned and looked right at him. "I wasn't planning on going out with anyone while I was here."

"Seems smart," he murmured, his eyes dropping to her mouth.

She giggled and swept up onto her toes to she could place a kiss on his cheek. "Yeah, I don't always do the smart thing. You should probably know that before things go too far." She settled back onto her feet and started walking again. Tingles raced through her body, and the message from her lips was that they wanted to touch his. Sure, his cheek was exciting, but only because it was so close to that mouth.

She ducked her head as if Gavin would be able to read her thoughts. They walked in silence for a block, and then

Navy said, "And I don't know if you've ever sat in on a matchmaking reading with your grandmother, but it isn't about the man at all. You should know that. It's about the woman. My reading was about *me*. Helping *me* to know how to make smarter dating decisions."

"Mm," he said.

"It was," she insisted.

He chuckled and released her hand so he could put his arm around her shoulders. He pulled her flush against him. "I believe you, Navy."

He sounded sincere, and Navy wanted him to say her name in his bass voice again. And again. Preferably just before he kissed her.

She glanced up and realized they'd walked from her cottage to his house. "Hey, that's the Old Main Hill Bed and Breakfast." She glanced at Gavin, who wore a distasteful expression. "Oh, come on," she said, pulling him across the street. "Be a little spontaneous."

"I'm spontaneous," he said.

"Prove it. Just walk around here with me. Let's look at it."

"You do realize I don't cook, right?"

"Did you even look at the link I sent you?"

"Of course I did. It doesn't look anything like this."

Navy took in the land before her. It was wild and unkept; the grass needed mowing and watering as it was already starting to yellow; the buildings seemed without spirit. "It just needs a little love," she said.

"And a chef," he muttered.

"I can cook," she said, moving toward a cabin that boasted a Texas star on the exterior.

Gavin stopped her by slipping his hand from her shoulder to hers and pulling. "Navy."

She turned back to him. "What?"

"Do you realize what you just said?"

She peered up at him, noting the seriousness, the concern. "I said I know how to cook."

"So...what? You're going to teach me? Or you're going to stay here in Three Rivers and be my cook?" He exhaled, his frustration evident. "You're a pediatric nurse from Dallas. You have a job and a family and a life there." He shook his head and released her hand. "I'm not—"

"If you say you're not interested, Gavin Redd, I'll... I'll...I don't know what I'll do, but it will be really bad."

He met her eye with passion and panic in his. "I *am* interested," he said in a low, husky voice. "That's the whole problem."

Navy edged a little closer to him and took both of his hands in hers. "Why is that a problem?"

"You're a pediatric nurse from Dallas. You have a job and a family and a life there. I don't date women who don't live in Three Rivers. I don't date women who've gone to see my grandmother. I don't date women who believe a coin in a wishing well will bring them the man of their dreams. I don't date, *period.*"

Though some of his words jabbed into the fleshy parts

of her heart, she smiled. Laughed—complete with the snort. "You've gotten crotchety in your old age."

"Old age?" His eyebrows went as high as his voice.

Navy sobered, a chilling thought occurring to her. "Do you really want to be alone for the rest of your life?"

His jaw worked and his eyes stormed. "No," he finally clipped out.

"Good," Navy said, stretching up again. "Me either." She put her hands on his shoulders to balance herself, a million watts of excitement and energy popping from her to him and back again. "I've kissed cowboys before," she whispered. "The hat is always in the way."

He removed it with one hand and steadied her with the other around her waist. But he didn't lean down the four inches he needed to in order to touch her lips with his.

"Are you going to kiss me or what?" she asked.

It seemed that those words finally broke down whatever barrier he'd put between them. Because he dropped his beloved cowboy hat, wrapped both arms around her, and kissed her like she'd never been kissed before.

His mouth was cool and he tasted like chocolate and mint. Navy couldn't get enough of him, and thankfully he seemed to feel the same about her as he prolonged the kiss.

# Chapter Fourteen

Gavin knew the moment his lips touched Navy's that he'd never kissed a woman like her. So full of spunk, and intelligence, and spirit. He held her tightly against him, never wanting her more than a few inches from him again.

He stroked his mouth over hers, glad when she responded eagerly. He moved his lips to her throat, which caused her to arch into him. His pulse raced and his breath came so quick, so quick.

After several seconds, he managed to calm himself and really enjoy the apple-y taste of her mouth, the swell of her hips against his palms, the presence of her so near him. When he finally pulled away and rested his forehead against hers, it was because he'd realized he was making out with her in a very public place.

"Wow," she whispered. "I'd really like to know how

you show a woman you're interested in her, if that's how you kiss someone you're *not* interested in."

Humiliation threaded through him. "Sometimes a person lies to themselves," he whispered back. "It's a defense mechanism you might be familiar with."

She trilled out a little laugh that drove him wild. "So you *are* interested."

He kissed her again. Kissed her until he felt sure his lips would bruise. Kissed her until she pulled away first. Then he said, "I like you, Navy Richards," in a voice that sounded like he'd gargled with glass.

Gavin enjoyed her smile, liked the way she deliberately put her hand in his, even went along with her when she said, "Let's look at this one first."

"You know," he said. "I don't think you can just look around here. We probably need to call a realtor."

"Probably," she said as she reached the porch where his granddad had rested last week. Navy gave Gavin a flirty smile and twisted the doorknob. Cooler air beckoned him inside, so Gavin followed, though he very much felt like he was trespassing.

"This one has a little kitchen. And look." She picked up a dust-covered piece of paper. "This is the Texas Railroad room."

Gavin took in the railroad crossing posts on either side of the stripped down bed. The whole place smelled musty, and old—a lot like his grandparents' house in the winter when they never opened the windows. He couldn't help the way his nose scrunched up.

"I can't imagine anyone would want to stay here," he said.

"Well, you'd clean it up, obviously." Navy put the laminated paper back on the kitchen counter. "I like it. It's nice. This is all cosmetic stuff, like what you're doing to my cabin." She walked over to a door and discovered a bathroom.

Gavin thought if he poured time, money, and energy into the bed and breakfast, it would probably match the pictures in the real estate listing Navy had sent over.

But just because there were cabins didn't make this place a ranch. Gavin wanted horses, and stables, and cows, and cowboys. He wanted wide open space and rustling prairie grasses. The Old Main Hill B&B had the wild grass part down, but it was literally one block away from down-town Three Rivers. Not exactly the kind of open space Gavin craved.

Still, he allowed Navy to lead him on an expedition through all eight cabins, as well as the main house. "You'd live here," she said with this perma-grin on her face that was starting to rub Gavin the wrong way.

"This is a *bed and breakfast*," he said for the umpteenth time.

She ignored him, just as she had been for the past hour. They eventually went back to her house, but Gavin didn't pick up with the painting. He lounged in the shade with her fingers held loosely in his, wondering if this might finally be the relationship that worked. Despite the fact that Navy had gone to see his grandmother and believed in the myths of Three Rivers.

No matter what, a sense of contentment had infected him. A feeling a peace he hadn't experienced in quite a long time. So he held on to that and wasted the afternoon talking with Navy and kissing Navy and hoping Navy wouldn't leave him high and dry the way everyone else had.

GAVIN PULLED the nail from between his lips and hammered it into the windowsill. How that had gotten broken was a mystery to him. Whoever had lived in this cabin before him must've had some really rowdy parties.

Probably why Squire suddenly needed a new cowhand.

The cabin out at Three Rivers Ranch wasn't anything spectacular, but it served as a place of refuge and rest for the cowboys who worked the ranch.

Gavin wondered if Navy could ever picture herself out here with him. The idea couldn't grow legs, because Gavin knew only the foreman got a larger cabin and was allowed a family.

He finished piecing the molding together for the windowsill, and he switched to sanding so he could paint next. The repairs on the cabin were almost finished, and then he could move in.

There were so many loose ends still in town, and he wondered again if this ranch was the right place for him to be.

He loved his time out here. It seemed like it was a patch of earth that was closer to the Lord than anywhere else on the planet. It was just so far away from his house, his grandparents...and Navy.

He'd been spending days fixing up this cabin and nights working at hers. She was great company, and he left a little bit drunk off her kisses every evening.

The door behind him opened, and he turned to see Squire walking in. "Hey, boss."

They shook hands and Squire took several moments to gaze around the place. "It's looking great."

"Yep." Gavin could see all the little things that didn't look great, but he kept those to himself.

"You think you'll be able to move out here when it's finished?"

"Yep, I've talked to my aunt about coming to take care of my grandparents. She might take them to Amarillo. It's still up in the air." He didn't mention the job at Navy's. That should be done in the next day or two, and it certainly didn't prevent him from his job out here.

"Great," Squire said. "Wondering if you'd take a break from this so I can show you our budgeting process."

"Sounds exciting." Gavin grinned and clapped the dust from the sanding off his hands.

Squire chuckled. "Hardly anything about ranch management is exciting, but you're the one with the degree, so you must like it."

Gavin followed the other man out of the cabin, which sat smack dab in the middle of the row. Six stretched to his right, and six sat on his left.

The heat hit him like a fiery fist in the throat, and he struggled to breathe for a moment. Then, as if his body remembered he lived in Texas, everything was fine.

"You're a vet, right?" he asked Squire as they walked down the rock path.

"That's right. I handle all the ranch animal medical needs. Pete's got someone part-time over there. And Brynn's looking for someone. We've also got Cal, who's my assistant on the ranch."

"Mm." Gavin nodded. The admin building was a hub of activity, with three men at desks, talking into radios. He hadn't met all the cowboys at the ranch yet, but he and Squire had been working on personnel board, and he knew Squire employed over thirty people just for the ranch need.

Three Rivers was a big ranch, and Gavin wondered if he should just stay here to fulfill his dreams of owning a ranch. Because whatever he'd be able to afford, it wouldn't be half this nice or even a quarter this big.

He focused as Squire went over the budget, absorbing

everything he could, whether for this job or a ranch of his own, it didn't matter. He needed to know it, so he focused and learned it.

When Squire finished, he pushed several papers together and put them in a folder for Gavin. A listing for a ranch sat on the desk, and Gavin asked, "What's that?"

Squire picked up the sheet of paper. "Oh, this is from Pete. There's an old ranch out here that borders mine. He thinks I should buy up the land and get more cattle." Squire tossed the paper back to the desk. "He feels bad about taking up a bunch of acres with his homestead and training facility."

"It is a huge facility," Gavin said. He'd never been inside, but the building itself said volumes. He nodded toward the paper. "Can I have that?"

"Are you lookin' to buy a ranch of your own?" He handed the paper to Gavin.

"I mean, I don't know." Gavin shrugged. "It's been a dream of mine."

Squire watched him, but Gavin couldn't tell what the other man was thinking. He folded the paper and tucked in his back pocket. "Thanks, Squire. I'll see you tomorrow."

"Yeah. Tomorrow."

Gavin left the ranch, the paper in his back pocket as heavy as a load of bricks. Did he really want to buy a piece of land? No cattle. No homestead. But a bare patch of land, with untold potential.

The idea was as intriguing as it was horrifying.

* * *

"WELL, THAT SHOULD DO IT." Gavin wiped his fingers along the countertop again just to make sure he'd gotten the last of the paint and dust grime. He glanced at Navy. "What do you think?"

"What do I think?" She turned in a circle inside her remodeled cottage, her face alight with wonder. "I think it's fantastic." She skipped over to him in the kitchen. "Just like you."

She kissed him quick and pulled away. He stood still, watching her with a small smile on his face. The past couple of weeks of working with her, kissing her, and much as he hadn't wanted to admit it, dating her, had been pretty great.

Navy fisted her fingers in his shirt and kissed him again, this time with double the passion. Gavin growled and pulled her closer, kissed her deeper. "Want to go to dinner in Amarillo?" he whispered just before tracing his teeth along her earlobe.

She clung to his shoulders in a needful way he adored, traced her fingernails along the hair on the back of his neck, and giggled as he trailed kisses down her throat. "Yes," she said, pushing fruitlessly against his collarbone to get him to stop. "But I don't want to go anywhere Asian."

"Still recovering from that sushi place?"

"There's a reason sushi shouldn't be served in the Texas panhandle." She disentangled herself from his arms. "You go shower, and I'll slip into that pink dress you like, and we'll go."

"Okay," he said. "But don't walk over. I'll come get you."

She paused in her retreat toward her bedroom. "Why can't I walk over?"

"It's probably a million degrees outside." He leaned against the counter. "Just let me come pick you up, would you?" She always walked over, and most of the time he found her on his grandparents' porch, waiting for him. He didn't like it. He wanted to pick her up for a date, the way a boyfriend would.

"Fine," she said. "I'll wait for you to pick me up." She grinned and ducked into her bedroom, which was Gavin's cue to leave. He hurried home, but before stepping into the shower, he went into his grandparents' home to check on them. The scent of roasting meat made his mouth water.

"Pork and potatoes," Grandmother said from where she sat in the recliner, doing her needlepoint. "Or are you going out with Navy again?"

Gavin leaned over and pecked Grandmother on the cheek. "Navy. Where's Granddad?"

"Out with the roses."

"It's too hot for that." Gavin looked toward the back of the house, but the walls kept him from spotting Granddad.

"He comes in every few minutes, muttering about spider mites."

"Make sure he drinks enough water."

Grandmother gave him a fast smile. "I will, dear."

"Have you heard from Aunt Ally this week?"

"She called last night." The needle went in and out, in and out. "She just started her last case, and her retirement timeline still looks good."

Gavin sat down, though he was risking Navy walking over here. "And you guys are okay with me moving out to Three Rivers Ranch? I mean, I'm still going to be nearby, but I won't be next door—"

"Gavin." Grandmother put her needlepoint down. "You've told us all of this, and we support you. We don't feel abandoned by you." She reached out and cradled his cheek in her weathered, wrinkled hand. "We love you, and we want you to go out there and work your ranch." She smiled, the warmth genuine in her still-sharp, blue eyes.

If only Three Rivers was his ranch, but he didn't correct her.

Gavin nodded, unsure as to why he needed this reassurance from her. He normally didn't question himself so much. But everything with Navy had shaken his confidence, and he didn't want to make mistakes. With her. With his life. Not anymore.

Simple fact: He was scared.

He stood and said, "I have to go shower. Thanks, Grandmother." He hurried through getting ready and feeding the dogs. They were probably out in the yard with Granddad, as none of them had shown up yet. He put their bowls in the shade and jumped in the truck.

His grandparents' front porch sat empty, and Gavin grinned. Navy sat in the grass at the end of her lane, though, still robbing Gavin of the opportunity to knock on her front door and pick her up properly.

He got out of the truck so he could open her door at least. "You walked," he said.

"Not all the way." She flashed him a smile, and he brushed his fingers through her hair, thrilled he could touch her so intimately now without worry.

"One of these days I'd like to come to your door, present you with roses or something, and kiss you hello."

Navy paused with one sandaled foot on the truck's runner. "What would the 'something' be?"

Gavin shrugged and boosted her into the truck. "Candy? Women like candy."

She laughed, her cute little snort breaking up the sound. "If I were you, and you were coming to pick me up, the something should be Diet Coke or cupcakes. Or both."

"Noted."

When Gavin got behind the wheel, Navy asked, "So what do you think of taking me fishing one of these weekends?"

He nearly drove off the road. "You want to go fishing with me?"

"You seem to really enjoy it." She scooted over next to

him and tucked herself into his side. "And you're gone for a really long time when you go. Maybe I could just read on the riverbank."

Gavin laughed and squeezed her hand. "If you want to come fishing, you can come."

"What about Steve?"

"Steve's a big boy. He can handle it. Or we'll go ourselves."

"So it's almost June. You said the fishing's good until then."

"So you're saying you want to go tomorrow?"

"Sure, great idea."

Gavin shook his head, knowing full-well that it wasn't his idea at all.

But the next morning found him packing up his fishing gear, a cooler full of food and bottled water, and his backpack with sunscreen and snacks for the road trip. His nerves seemed shaky, and he finally realized it was because he was sharing something important to him with Navy, who had also become important to him.

He showed up at her house early and got out to knock. She opened the door almost instantly and said, "I waited for you to come all the way to the door." She glanced at his hands and clucked her tongue. "And no cupcakes. This is why I walk."

He burst into laughter and swept her off her feet and into his arms. He righted her and pressed his lips to hers.

"Good morning," he murmured between kisses. "How's the curtain rod holding up?"

"Fine," she said breathlessly, holding onto him even when he started to release her.

The trip to Lake Meredith seemed to pass in a moment, with times of silence, times full of conversation and laughter, times where Navy sang really loudly to the song on the radio. Gavin enjoyed every moment, glad they could exist in silence sometimes and be comfortable inside their own heads.

"You can camp here?" Navy peered through the windshield as Gavin pulled into the Lake Meredith RV Camp.

"Sure," he said.

"Do you ever do that?"

"Haven't for years," he said. "Steve likes to go home to his family at night."

"We fish here?"

He pulled into a parking spot at the RV office. "I have to get the day passes, and then we'll go down the bank a bit. You'll see people swimming and stuff, and we'll want to be a little ways from them."

He ran inside and bought their passes while Navy looked around like she'd never been inside a campground office gift shop before. "Look at this bear!" she exclaimed, holding up a saltshaker shaped like a black bear.

Gavin's heart softened at the sight of her. So blonde. So smart. So exuberant about a black bear saltshaker.

Everything inside him turned to mush, and Gavin recognized the feelings, as he'd felt them before.

This was the first inklings of love, and he twisted back to the cash register so she wouldn't see it shining in his eyes. He swallowed as he thanked the camp manager and took his fishing passes.

He'd never been as scared as he was in that moment. That single moment before he turned around and found Navy stroking a stuffed sunfish with a giant smile on her face.

# Chapter Fifteen

Everything about Lake Meredith and fishing was new to Navy. She felt like a child experiencing things for the first time. Gavin taught her how to hook on the bait, how to cast out her line. She couldn't do it at all, but he was kind and patient, and she certainly didn't hate how he stood behind her, a wall of solid muscle, as he explained once again how to hold the rod.

Eventually, she wandered back to the shore and just watched him cast and reel in. Cast and reel in. It seemed impossible that a fish would be able to latch onto the hook, but Gavin pulled in half a dozen fish in an hour's time.

Gavin waded in and rested his pole next to hers against the tree where she'd set up their camp chairs. "You okay?"

"Best day ever." She grinned. "Well, maybe. What have you got in the cooler?"

"Let's see." He sighed as he sat down and opened the cooler. "This one's an old family recipe." He pulled out a sandwich made on a round roll instead of two pieces of bread. "I'm not sure you'll like it, so I'll keep that one." He put it on his lap and started to dig in the cooler again.

"Wait a second," she said. "What is it? I like old family recipes."

He gave her a wary look. "It's a spam and egg sandwich. Pickles. Mayo. It's sort of like egg salad, but with spam."

Navy couldn't think of anything more repulsive. Well, besides grape-flavored things.

"And I'll keep it." Gavin chuckled as he went back to the cooler. "Told you you wouldn't like it."

"I want to try it."

"I packed that turkey and Swiss you like." He produced a sandwich made on regular wheat bread and dangled it in front of her.

"Gavin, I want to try the spam and egg."

"All right." He passed her the roll and watched with amusement as she opened the sandwich bag.

The scent of pickle and mayo and egg hit her when she opened it, and her stomach squirmed. She wasn't exactly a vegetarian, but she didn't eat red meat. She withdrew the sandwich and took a big bite, her eyes locked on Gavin's.

She chewed, the taste salty from the spam and acidic

from the pickle. "It's not bad." She passed the sandwich back to him.

He glanced at it and then looked back at her. "So now I have to eat it with a bite taken out of it?"

She slapped his knee. "You kiss me. I think you can handle eating a sandwich I bit off of."

He muttered something under his breath as he rebagged the sandwich and tossed it into the cooler.

"What was that?" she asked in a teasing tone.

"I want my whole sandwich," he said in a clear voice. For a moment, she thought he was mad about the bite, but when he looked at her, she found the mischievous glint in his eye. He reached for her and kissed her, really taking his time to explore her mouth.

She melted into him, a feeling of safety and a rush of adrenaline pouring through her. She really liked Gavin, and she wasn't quite sure what to do about it. It had only been a few weeks since they'd met, but she felt like she'd known him for years. She trusted him in a way she hadn't trusted a man in a long time.

Navy couldn't make sense of how comfortable she felt with Gavin. She suspected the fact that he met some of his grandmother's advice for who Navy should be with had a lot to do with it. And she wasn't sure if she liked that or not.

Gavin broke their kiss with a massive grin on his face. "All right." He pulled out some bottled water and her diet cola. "Drinks. And I have grapes and cheese sticks. Oh, and chips." He opened his backpack and pulled out two bags of chips.

They ate in silence, the picturesque lake before them. Navy snapped a photo of the landscape and then a selfie of her and Gavin. He fished the afternoon away and she napped, read, and spent an unhealthy amount of time watching him.

She finally waded out to try fishing again, the water cool against her legs. She failed at the fishing, so she took her pole back to the tree. She got back in the water just to stay cool and to be nearer to Gavin.

Navy inched closer to him, careful to stay out of range of his casting arm. She took a step and her ankle twisted. She yelped at the same time she went down, flailing to grab onto him.

Next thing she knew, water splashed in her face, up her nose, and then Gavin landed next to her. More water cascaded over her, causing her to sputter as she tried to figure out how she'd ended up on her backside, fully dressed, in the lake.

She looked at Gavin, who had water dripping from the brim of his cowboy hat as well as his nose. "Sorry," she said just before she started laughing.

He joined her, the sound of their combined voices lifting into the sky. She snorted, but she couldn't help herself. Gavin slung his soaking wet arm around her shoulder and squeezed her. "Is that your way of saying it's time to go?"

"No, I swear...." She couldn't speak through her laughter. She and Gavin sat in the water, chuckling for several more moments, and Navy thought there couldn't be anything better. No one she'd dated in the last five years would be happy she'd pulled them into the lake. None of those men even liked fishing, and Navy had never found herself going on many outdoor dates.

But sitting there in Lake Meredith with Gavin felt like the most natural thing in the world. Navy took a few seconds to bask in the knowledge of that and let it settle into her mind. Then she put her hand in Gavin's and allowed him to help her stand.

"Let's get packed up, and then we'll go find some ice cream," he said, and Navy swore he was speaking her love language. At the very least, he'd been paying attention all these weeks, and that made her feel cherished.

JUNE PASSED with waves of heat, and lazy days reading while Gavin worked, and sultry summer nights in various small Texas towns scattered across the panhandle—and even up into Oklahoma. Gavin took her to music festivals, and barbecue tastings, and dances. And the man could *dance*.

Navy woke up the day after Independence Day and practically bolted from bed. "Death by Chocolate Week." She'd already packed her bags; they'd been waiting by the front door for days. She'd found the event three hours from Three Rivers several weeks ago, and Gavin had made their hotel arrangements.

She'd never been so excited for something in her entire life. An all-you-can-eat chocolate chip pancake breakfast. Chocolate tastings all day long, for days. And a chocolate slip-n-slide. Not that Navy would be doing that, but she couldn't wait to watch the kids.

*Lynn texted with a This week is your first trip with Gavin, yes? I want details!*

Navy had been very thorough about keeping her friend up to date on the progression of their relationship. She needed someone impartial to talk to about the legend of Three Rivers, and that certainly wasn't Gavin. They hadn't spoken of his distaste for the history of his home-town, and she hadn't brought up anything concerning astrological signs.

Lynn gave her advice when she needed it. She didn't judge. She simply offered her friendship and support, and as Navy hadn't really made any friends in town, her communication with Lynn was really important to her.

*I'm super nervous, Navy texted.*

*About what?*

*That he'll be sick of me after one day.* She twirled the owl ring on her pinky finger, her nerves parading through her like a marching band.

*He hasn't gotten sick of you yet.*

*He lived out on the ranch now, and we see each other for an hour or two at night. But this week it's just us.*

*Just keep doing what you're doing, Lynn texted. Or don't. Do something different. You've done lots of things differently with Gavin, and it's working out.*

Navy felt the truth of Lynn's words, and she smiled as she thumbed out *Thank you.*

Gratitude filled her, but she jumped when Gavin knocked on the door. Her heart leapt into her throat and she hurried to the door. Gavin stood on the other side wearing his trademark jean shorts and somehow he made every T-shirt look sexy, even faded gray ones with the outline of Texas and the words IT'S BETTER HERE in all caps. He had his head bowed so all she could see was the top of his cowboy hat.

"Hey." She backed into the house so he could enter.

He lifted his eyes to hers, and her breath seized in her lungs. He was so handsome, and so charming, and absolutely everything she wanted in a partner. Her heart tapped and then started drumming in her chest as she realized she was in love with him. Maybe not very far, but the "in-love" door had been opened and she'd stepped through it.

"Hey, yourself." He filled the doorframe and came inside.

She threw herself into his arms, laughed, and released her anxiety. Now that he was here, she couldn't believe she was worried about spending time with him. He twirled her around the way a strong cowboy boyfriend should before setting her on her feet and kissing her properly.

When he broke their connection, he said, "I was worried about this week," he said. "But I'm not sure why."

"You were?"

"Yeah." He emitted a nervous chuckle. "Silly, right?"

"No, I was a nervous wreck this morning even though I've had my bags packed for days."

She watched him lick his lips before he spoke, one of his mannerisms she adored. "I'm glad it wasn't just me." He reached for her suitcases.

"What were you nervous about?"

"Everything."

"We've taken a road trip before."

"I know."

"We have separate rooms in Lubbock."

"I know." She followed him out to the truck, where he tossed her bags in the back. "Why were you nervous?"

Navy tucked her hair behind her ear and turned to survey the expansive lawn between her cottage and the Shepherd's house. "It's silly."

"Tell me anyway."

"I'm worried you'll get sick of me after a week together without a break."

His fingers tripped along hers. "That is silly."

"Believe it or not, I've heard it before."

"You've gone on week-long trips with men in the past?"

"You've been engaged," she said. "You never took a trip together?"

He shook his head, a dark look in his eye. "No, Joan wouldn't leave Three Rivers for longer than a few hours."

"Well, it's a major step in a relationship." Navy slipped her free hand to the back of his neck and played with the hair there.

"How so?"

Navy shrugged, glad when he released her hand and held her close to his chest. "We'll basically be together all day and most of the night for the next five days. It's intense. I don't know. It's...intense."

His pulse picked up, and Navy smiled against the fabric of his shirt. "But it's gonna be fine." She pushed out of his arms. "More than fine. Fun. I mean, it's five days of *chocolate*. So let's go."

# Chapter Sixteen

Any concerns Gavin had about taking a five-day trip with his girlfriend were eradicated within the first hour of travel. Things between him and Navy were easy, casual, comfortable. After their initial excitement, she pulled out her e-reader and he turned up the radio. He imagined their life together being this carefree, and he started singing along to the country song blasting through the cab.

After several songs, Navy reached over and turned the volume down. "You really are a fantastic singer. Tell me what happened to ruin that."

Gavin glanced at her, and part of him wanted her to know everything about him. Wasn't that what couples did? Shared their lives—the good, the bad, and the ugly—with each other?

He took a deep breath, his nerves dancing again. "So

the first woman who came to Three Rivers with a bus ticket and all her hopes hinging on finding her match—her name was Debbie. She was blonde, petite, a real firecracker." Gavin thought of the woman; the first woman he'd really fallen for.

"She knew exactly what she wanted, and most of the time, she got it. She met with Grandmother, and I happened to be moving in next door."

"So this was a while ago."

"Oh, about eleven years now." Gavin sighed. He couldn't believe he'd been making the same mistakes with women for so long. Or that he'd stayed in Three Rivers for so long. A saner man would've been driven out of his hometown by now.

"Anyway, Grandmother told her she should be looking for someone who could sing, and somehow, that's what Debbie seized on." He thought about what Navy had said about her match reading. How it was for *her*, and not about a man at all. He wondered if that was really true.

"So she showed up at church that Sunday and moved all over the chapel. I didn't find out until later that she was listening to the men who were singing. Apparently I was one of the best, because she asked me out." He shrugged. "Honestly, I was flattered. So I went out with her. She dated three of us that summer—unbeknownst to any of us —and encouraged us all to sign up for this singing competition in Amarillo." He chuckled, glad he could talk about this disaster without getting angry or feeling humiliated. He used to do both.

"So I show up at this competition, and there's these two other guys standing with Debbie. She's smoothing down one's shirt and fixing another's hair. I figured things out pretty darn quick after that."

"Did you sing?"

"No way."

"So she broke up with you."

"I never saw her again. Apparently, whoever won the contest was going to be her choice and she was going to propose. She never came back to Three Rivers at all."

"Wow."

"Yeah." Gavin released a breath, released a portion of the negativity he'd carried for that particular blonde. "I call that the Debbie Debacle."

"And yet you went out with another blonde, another woman who met with your grandmother."

"I can't seem to fix my mistakes."

"Hey." She slugged him, and he laughed.

He laced his fingers through hers. "I guess I just keep hoping that one of these times, I really will be the man someone wants."

"Stop it." Navy laid her head against his bicep. "You're a great person."

He noticed she didn't say she wanted him, but Gavin trusted his feelings. And she kissed him all the time, sat right next to him in the truck, seemed happy and comfortable with him. Her actions spoke louder than her saying he was the man for her.

At least he hoped they did.

* * *

ACTIVITY AND SUNLIGHT doused Gavin's senses. They'd parked—quite a ways away too—and paid to get into the five-day Death by Chocolate event. "This is insane," he said, glancing around. "Where do we even start?"

"Let's see." Navy studied a pamphlet she'd been given. "Do we want to attend the cooking demos? There are tastings afterward. Or we can head over to the big tent, where they're doing chocolate crafts in about forty-five minutes." She glanced up, her eyebrows drawn into a V as she made sense of where she was. "There will be booths along here. We can just wander."

"I think the tastings sound fun," he said.

"Me too." She pointed to her left. "They're doing mini lava cakes in fifteen minutes."

"I've never said no to a lava cake."

Navy giggled, secured her hand in his, and strolled with him toward a blessedly air conditioned building which was almost full already. They managed to find seats on the side with a decent view, and Gavin enjoyed himself as the culinary instructor whipped up a cake batter and slid two dozen cakes into the oven.

"And you want to make sure you time them exactly,"

the woman said. "No more than twenty-three minutes." She pulled a tray out of another oven. "You'll be tempted to leave them in longer. But look, we want the middle to be liquid." She poked one of the cakes. "See how it jiggles, just a little? That's what you want."

Two assistants came from the door behind the demo area, carrying trays of cakes. The instructor said, "Come get one, and there are recipes online. You can scan this code, and it'll email it to you."

Gavin had never seen people rush a counter before, and he actually feared for the instructor. A line formed after the initial surge, and he and Navy waited to get their lava cake. He thought sure they'd run out, but the assistants kept bringing more and more, and he and Navy both got one. She scanned the recipe code, and they stepped out onto the shaded lawn beside the building.

"That was awesome," she said, breaking into her cake with her plastic fork. "Look! Mine's oozing."

Gavin beamed at her exuberance. Being with her, watching her childlike excitement, thinking of all he knew about her, Gavin realized how much he liked her. In fact, he may have crossed over from like to love.

"Have you talked to your parents?" he asked.

"Yeah, I called them a couple of days ago. They're still worried about me being up here all alone."

He ate his lava cake while she talked about her younger brother, who'd apparently just asked his girlfriend to marry him. "Mom says I have to be home by the wedding, and I told her of course I would be." Navy put her empty plate in the trashcan. "Am I bad person if I say I don't want to attend the wedding? It's just...." She got that faraway look on her face she often did when she spoke of things that reminded her of what she didn't have.

The fact that Gavin knew that made his heart sing. "It'll be hard for you," he said. "But not because you're not happy for him. But because you want to be married too."

"Yes, exactly." She looked at him. "Mom said they won't even get married until next summer, so it's not like I won't be back in time."

His heart somersaulted. "Of course you will be." He sounded like he was choking on the last bite of his cake, but Navy didn't seem to notice. "Do you miss your job?"

"A little." She sighed. "Actually, not that much. I mean, I love taking care of the babies. I just...it's so nice not to work for fourteen hours. Nice to sleep at night when most people do. Nice to just...be." She gazed into the sky and then pulled out the event pamphlet again. "There's another demo in twenty minutes. Chocolate dipping."

Gavin tossed his trash in the same can she had. "Let's go then."

"I bet they'll do fruit," she said. "Which is just a crime. Fruit and chocolate do not go together."

"No?" Gavin had gotten used to some of her food quirks. She liked onion rings, but not onions. She liked blueberries as long as they were cooked into something like muffins or pancakes. Otherwise, no. She disliked anything grape-flavored, including grape juice, but grapes themselves were tolerable.

"No." She shook her head. "Those chocolate oranges everyone gives at Christmas? Disgusting."

"I like them."

"You like everything."

"That's not true."

"Name one thing."

"I think plain vanilla ice cream is a crime. No one should consume that, under any circumstances."

Navy took one step and then burst into laughter, complete with her cute little snorting every few beats. Gavin tucked her against his side and pressed a kiss to her temple, falling all the way over the like line and into love.

A blip of anxiety squirreled through him, but nothing like he'd experienced before. He really wanted—*needed*—her to be different from the other women who'd come to Three Rivers.

*She is*, a voice whispered in his head, and he seized onto it.

*Please let her be*, he prayed, unable to come up with anything else.

By the end of the week, Gavin had tasted more chocolate desserts than he'd thought humanly possible. Navy's favorite was the chocolate baklava. His was the chocolate-dipped cherries, which she'd also deemed "awful" just before spitting it into the trash. At least she'd tried it.

They'd eaten their fair share of chocolate chip pancakes on the final day of the festival, and Navy had insisted they stay to watch the children slide face-first down a sheet of plastic covered in melted chocolate. Gavin had to admit he'd never seen anything like it.

He'd never done anything like the Death by Chocolate Week at all. Never gone away with a woman like that. Never wanted a woman the way he wanted Navy.

Back in Three Rivers, he had a mountain of paperwork on his desk in the admin trailer, and the task of hiring two more cowboys as a couple had quit while he'd been gone.

Squire was in a foul mood because he'd had to deal with all kinds of management issues while Gavin had been tasting chocolate covered raisins, so Gavin kept his head down and got the job done.

At lunchtime, he took a few precious minutes to check the real estate listings for ranches in the area. He'd been looking every few days to see if anything new came up, and today there were two new cattle ranches.

His heart ba-bumped in anticipation as he scanned the info. Both were in his price range. One was located about forty minutes southwest of Three Rivers, which was an easy distance to travel to check on his grandparents if he needed to.

The ranch was only five hundred acres, and only two thousand head of cattle. But it was a ranch Gavin could afford. It boasted a nice-sized homestead, with two barns, a stable, silos, and three cowboy cabins. He wanted to see it in person, see if he could feel God's presence in the wind at Dripping Springs Ranch, so he clicked the "Request Showing" button and put in his information.

The paper he'd taken a couple of weeks ago simply was land, and he'd decided that was too much work. He didn't have time or resources to build a house, a barn, a corral, the cows, any of it.

The other ranch was also in his price range—but for a reason. It had been abandoned a year ago, and needed some serious work to get it functioning again. The three thousand head of cattle had been looked after by a neighboring ranch, and the funds to keep paying him had run out.

"Seems like the B&B," Gavin muttered as he read. Family-owned and operated. Down on their luck. Sold a bunch of cattle and equipment to try to salvage things, but in the end, it was simply time to let go.

"Might as well go see it too," Gavin said. The ranch was in farther west in Texas, closer to the New Mexico border than he liked. He clicked the button, put in his info, and finished the day in the trailer. As he drove to Navy's for a home-cooked meal, his phone rang.

He answered it, and it was the realtor for the first ranch. "When can you come?" she asked.

"When works for you? Evenings are best for me," Gavin said. "I manage a ranch in Three Rivers."

"Tomorrow night? Seven o'clock?"

"I'll be there." Feeling warm and happy and like maybe his dreams could come true, Gavin hung up. He couldn't wait to tell Navy about the ranch. He didn't even knock, just burst into her house.

She twirled from her position at the stove. "What's going on?" She abandoned whatever she was cooking and came toward him, a concerned expression on her face.

"Nothing." He grinned at her and kissed her quick. "But I just scheduled to go see a ranch tomorrow night. Will you come with me?"

# Chapter Seventeen

Navy blinked at Gavin. He'd found a ranch? And not only that, he wanted her at his side when he went to look at it. She loved that he'd included her in his life so intimately.

"Of course I'll go with you." She stretched up and kissed him. "Where is it? Do you have the website?"

He swiped and tapped and typed and showed her the listing. "It's small," he said. "But I can't afford big. I should probably face that fact."

"It's nice." She swiped right to see more pictures. "Look at those barns. Those look great." She glanced up but didn't really focus on Gavin before returning her attention to the ranch. She finished, a warm feeling extending down her arms and making her smile swift. "Dripping Springs Ranch. It looks awesome, Gavin."

He took his phone back, and she rushed over to the

stove, where she'd left the grits. She stirred the gloopy mess and it came back together with a bit of extra cream. Gavin's arms snaked around her from behind, and she giggled.

"Smells good."

"I made beef Bolognese and grits."

"I don't know what Bolognese is, but I heard beef and grits." He pressed a kiss on her neck and tightened his grip on her body.

"Behave yourself." She swatted at his strong arm, but he didn't move an inch.

"I am." He kissed her again, this time closer to her ear.

She twisted off the heat under the grits and turned in his arms to properly kiss him. She felt something new in his touch, and she poured the same passion and emotion into hers.

"Navy," he said, his voice hoarse and husky.

"Yeah?"

"Nothing." He backed up a step.

She knew it wasn't nothing, but Gavin seemed ultra-interested in the grits, so she said, "Let's eat," and transferred the pot to the kitchen counter where the Bolognese already waited. She lifted the lid on the Dutch oven, and Gavin groaned.

"I think *you* should buy the bed and breakfast," he said. "You could actually run it."

Navy smiled and dished herself dinner, her thoughts suddenly running wild. She'd never wanted to own a business, especially not something that required so much cleaning and cooking and care.

But she needed to find a reason to stay in Three Rivers. Stay with Gavin. And this town was lovely and charming, but it only had one hospital. One emergency clinic. Two doctor's offices, and that was it. Navy had spent the morning checking into all the staffing needs at each place, because the thought of leaving Three Rivers without Gavin made her heart shrivel.

* * *

THE FOLLOWING EVENING, she met Gavin at the bottom of his grandparents' stairs. "I couldn't wait," she explained. "Don't be mad."

He finished tucking his hair under his hat and ran his hand along his beard. "I'm not mad."

"Nervous?"

"A little."

"They're the ones who want you to buy the ranch."

"I looked at it again last night after I left your place." He opened the driver's side door and helped her up. "And again this morning. And again just now."

She trilled out a quick little laugh. "That's normal."

"Is it?" He got behind the wheel and started the truck. "Doesn't feel normal." He turned up the volume on the radio, and Navy let him disappear inside his head. She'd learned over the past few months that sometimes Gavin just needed to be. No conversation. No advice.

The drive to Dripping Springs Ranch took them straight across the panhandle, and Navy admired the landscape as they left Three Rivers in their rear-view mirror. "That sign said something about the Tri State Fair."

"Yeah." Gavin flexed his fingers on the wheel but didn't continue the conversation. "It's in Amarillo in September."

*You won't be here in September*, Navy thought, frowning. Yes, she would. She wasn't supposed to be back to work until November first. Her thoughts turned poisonous, worsening with every passing mile.

She tried to fight against the doomsday nature of her thoughts, but she couldn't win. The fact remained that she didn't live in Three Rivers. She wasn't engaged to Gavin. And she would be leaving in only three months.

*So what's the point?* she thought. *You can't hurt him the way those other women did.* The very idea made her chest collapse onto her lungs. She couldn't breathe as he turned down a smaller, grittier road and said, "We're almost there."

*Almost there* echoed in her mind. Was she "almost there" with him? Or had she been holding back because she knew she wasn't a permanent part of Three Rivers, of Gavin's life, of anything?

He turned right and then left, easing the truck onto a road that led west for a mile or two. "There it is."

The sign hanging in the field along the highway said, "Dripping Springs Ranch," and it seemed to fit exactly what Navy had envisioned for Gavin. They went down the dirt road to the homestead, which seemed to spread across the land, welcoming all who came that way.

"This looks nice." Gavin swallowed before getting out of the truck. So distracted was he, that he didn't turn back and offer his hand to Navy. She slid out of the truck and hovered a half-step behind him.

"It sure does." She inserted a false note of brightness into her voice so he wouldn't know she'd spent the last hour of their drive with doubts assaulting her.

A sharp dressed woman came out of the house, wearing a dark pantsuit. Navy thought she must be roasting under all the black fabric. A man followed her wearing blue jeans, a gray polo, and a white cowboy hat. Two dogs came with him, one on each side. "You must be Gavin." He shook Gavin's hand. "I'm Jake. Welcome to Dripping Springs Ranch." He flicked his eyes to Navy.

"This is my girlfriend," Gavin said, reaching for Navy's hand, which she willingly gave him. He squeezed it a bit too tight, an indication of his nerves. "Navy."

"Nice to meet you." Jake shook her hand too, and then exhaled as he glanced at the woman.

"This is our ranch real estate agent, Stephanie. She'll be givin' you the royal tour."

Stephanie smiled and tucked her dark hair behind her ear. She shook Gavin's hand and then Navy's. "Do you want Jake to come along? He might be able to answer more questions than I can."

"Sure," Gavin said, already scrutinizing the barn to his right.

Navy determined to keep quiet and keep her eyes open. Jake explained how the operation had been running, and Gavin asked questions about auctions, vaccinations, who was already on staff. He sounded very professional, very much like he'd run a cattle ranch before, which of course, he had. Navy basked in the sound of his voice, the way he conducted himself so well.

Stephanie led the tour inside the barns and the stable, the cowboy cabins—two of which were occupied by real, working cowboys. She explained when air conditioners had been replaced, and when carpet had been cleaned. They took a four-wheeler out to the fields, but Navy never did see a cow.

"They're out in the pastures," Jake explained. "We don't round 'em up until oh, November or so. Sometimes later."

Stephanie led them into the house, and it was clear a feminine hand had been taking care of the place. It smelled like lemons and antiseptic; classic art hung on the walls; big red flowers sat in the middle of the dining room table.

"My mother died," Jake explained once they'd gone through the expansive homestead. Navy had counted six bedrooms, and that seemed a little excessive to her.

"That's why we're selling." Jake glanced at a family photo above the TV. "Dad doesn't want to live here without her, and with his bad hip, he can't get as much done as he used to anyway."

"You don't want the ranch?" Gavin asked.

"I have my own," Jake said. "Five miles or so down the road. Butts right up against this property on the west."

Gavin nodded, his lips pressed into a tight line. Navy hadn't been able to get a read on him during the tour. She'd noticed how his gaze swept everything, took in each detail of each space. But he wore a mask so tight that she wondered if his head hurt from holding it in place.

"We're askin' one-point-seven million," Stephanie said. "Do you have an agent?"

"No, ma'am," Gavin said.

"It's no problem." She gave him a winning smile and retrieved a packet from the kitchen counter. "Here's everything we just went over. It's a big piece of property, with a lot of moving parts. I'm sure you'll want some time to consider everything."

Gavin took the glossy white folder. "Yeah, definitely."

"My card's inside." Stephanie started toward the exit. "So please let me know if you have any questions." She gestured them out of the house, and they left Jake and his two dogs behind.

Gavin headed toward the truck, but turned back. "Can I just...can I walk out to the end of the road again?"

Stephanie nodded and waved for him to go on. "Sure thing."

"Gavin?" Navy asked as he focused his attention along the road that went in front of the barns, the stable, the chicken coops.

"I just need to think." He released her hand, and she let him go down the lane alone. He made strong, sure steps, and he never looked back.

Navy wrapped her arms around herself though it was over a hundred degrees. Because she knew she wasn't the only one with doubts, and that the drive back to Three Rivers wouldn't be a silent one.

# Chapter Eighteen

Gavin loved Dripping Springs Ranch. He hadn't even made it to the end of the path yet when that peace he'd been searching for descended on him. He couldn't entirely describe it, but he knew he should do what he could to buy the ranch.

The slight breeze made the heat slightly more bearable but not by much. Confusion riddled Gavin's thoughts so he couldn't make sense of them.

He tried to think of a prayer, but he'd already uttered everything he needed help with. The Lord knew what was going on with Gavin and Navy; He knew what Gavin wanted, what he needed. He hoped it was Navy, didn't know what he'd do if she left him the way everyone else had.

Several minutes passed with the scent of dust in his nose and the whisperings of the wind in his ears. He didn't know what to do about Navy, but he did know he should put in an offer on this ranch.

Navy's touch as she slipped her arm into his made him look at her. "Hey."

"What are you thinking about?" she asked.

"Life and stuff."

She gave him a few more moments of silence. "Us?"

"Definitely us," he whispered.

Navy kept her eyes forward on the horizon. "Do you think we can make this work?"

"I want to believe we can," he said with a sigh. "But you live and work in Dallas, and I'm going to buy this ranch."

"You are?"

He nodded, wishing he could feel something besides defeat at the fact that she was still planning to return to Dallas, that she hadn't contradicted what he'd said.

"Let's go home," he said.

She went with him, but he sensed a Texas-sized storm brewing beneath her surface. Sure enough, they'd barely made it back to the main highway before Navy said, "Gavin, I like you, but—"

"Stop it," he said. "I don't want to talk about this today."

"Well, I do."

Gavin knew he couldn't make her stay silent, and that she'd do what she wanted. It was actually one of her best qualities—when it wasn't in contrast to what he wanted.

He slid her a look out of the corner of his eye. "And there's a lot more goin' on here than 'like,' Navy."

"Well, I—" she sputtered.

"For me," he clarified. "I think I've moved on from like, and I guess I'll just go ahead and ask."

She squeaked, but he continued anyway with, "What do you think about moving up here? Surely there's a clinic or a hospital or something who could use a nurse like you."

She exhaled a shaky laugh. "Oh, that's a different question than what I was expecting."

A few seconds passed before Gavin understood. "You thought I was going to ask you to marry me?"

"You just said this was more than *like* for you."

"You didn't say it back. You think I'd go from that to *marry me, Navy*?" He scoffed. "Not likely. There won't be any rings until I'm sure you'll show up at the wedding."

"I am *not* Joan," she snapped, folding her arms.

"I never said you were."

"You sometimes treat me like I'm all of them. Like because I want you to sing that I'm Debbie. Or because I'm blonde that I'll stomp on your heart the way Tabitha did." She moved over on the bench seat, putting inches of physical space between them and miles of emotional distance. "But I'm not any of them, Gavin. And this is never going to work until you realize that."

"I do realize that," he said.

"I don't think you do."

"You can think what you want."

"I will."

The conversation had sunk to a bad place, so Gavin clamped his mouth shut. No need to say anything he'd regret later. Navy wasn't listening anyway. He kept the speed at ten over the limit, the silence between them charged with emotion.

By the time he pulled into town, he'd relaxed but they still hadn't said much more than, "Are you hungry?" and "No."

He pulled into her long driveway and drove to the end. "Navy," he said.

"The ranch is wonderful," she said. "I hope you can buy it." She reached for the door handle.

"Will you at least think about what I asked?"

She finally met his eye, and he saw the same storm of indecision, of desire to do the right thing, of confusion, in her expression that he felt in every bone in his body.

"I've already been thinking about it." She opened the door and slid from the truck. "Call me tomorrow?"

He nodded and she disappeared into her cottage. Gavin watched the closed door for a few extra moments, almost hoping she'd come back out and profess her undying love for him, and say that of course she'd call her boss tomorrow and quit.

His reality was so different from his fantasies. He backed out onto the street and went home alone, the same way he'd been doing for the past forty years.

* * *

Gavin couldn't bring himself to call her the next day. He worked at his desk all day long and sent Navy a few texts during lunchtime. She took her sweet time responding, and when his phone sounded he nearly fell off his chair.

She hadn't responded to anything he'd said, but had texted *Dinner tonight?*

He couldn't help smiling at her invitation. She was always so quick to forgive. Always the one to ask to see him again. He really liked that about her. No, he *loved* that about her.

*Sure, he said. Are you cooking again?*

*No, I was thinking you could take me to the steakhouse.*

He frowned, his thumbs flying as he typed, *You don't like red meat.*

She didn't even address his concern. Simply asked, *Pick me up at six-thirty?*

Frustration and annoyance sang through him. He didn't want her going to the steakhouse because she thought it was something he'd like. He didn't need her babying him because he'd been unlucky in love in the past.

He glanced up from his phone and stumbled as if lightning had struck him. She'd been doing things to please him all this time. Walking over to his grandparents' house. Going fishing. Texting invitations.

Gavin blinked, trying to decide if her doing nice things

for him mattered. *Of course it matters!* he thought. *Do you even know her at all?*

He wasn't sure. And that made him angry.

*I have something to tell you,* she sent next. *Six-thirty?*

*Six-thirty is fine.* He sent the message and drew in a deep breath, his heart hammering now. He kept very still, waiting for the adrenaline to wear off. When it finally did, a sense of dread took its place.

Navy had something to talk to him about? He knew what that meant, had been through enough break-ups to know. His heart felt like he'd put it through a shredder, because he was seriously considering not showing up to take her to dinner. *But then you'll be a coward,* he thought.

And Gavin Redd was no coward. If Navy Richards was going to break up with him, she'd have to do it to his face while they ate red meat. He might even get grape soda so she'd know how much she didn't affect him.

At precisely six-thirty, he pulled into her driveway. Went all the way to the door. Knocked and waited. She took several long seconds to answer, and when she did, she was putting in her earrings. "Hey." She smiled at him, but didn't step into him, didn't kiss him, didn't giggle and throw herself into his arms the way she had countless times before.

She seemed distracted, distant. She was definitely breaking up with him. When she finally focused on him, he said, "We don't have to go out."

Navy tucked her hair and smiled, but it didn't hold its

usual wattage. Didn't even reach her eyes. "I have some news I want to discuss with you. It requires a huge plate of salad, and everyone in town says the steakhouse has the best salad bar."

"I forgot about your stress-eating-salad thing."

She took her hand in his, further confusing him. "I don't see how that's possible." She led him out of the cottage and he helped her into the truck. They arrived at the steakhouse, got a table, and she got her salad bar plate stacked full before saying another word.

She speared a broccoli floret and smeared it around in the ranch dressing. She stuck it in her mouth and chewed, swallowed. "My boss asked me to come back early."

Gavin had just torn off a piece of a wheat roll, but now his hands froze in midair. "When?"

"She called today. Said three nurses have quit, and she needs me back as soon as possible."

His throat felt like someone had lit a match and forced him to swallow it. Every rib in his chest cinched. He didn't want her to leave in three months, and she was going to leave *now*?

"What should I do?" She stuffed another bite of salad into her mouth.

Gavin put his bread on his plate, his hands trembling the tiniest bit. "I can't tell you that, Navy."

Tears formed in her eyes, but she just kept eating. Lettuce, cheese, cauliflower, croutons. He finally reached across the table and gently took her fork from her. A single tear trailed down her face, and she swiped it away.

"I love you," she said in a voice choked with emotion. "But my gut is telling me to go to Dallas and get back to work."

Gavin felt like someone had stabbed him with a steak knife. The warm gush of blood rushed through him, out of him, and he couldn't even enjoy the fact that she'd just told him she loved him.

"My brain says I'm an idiot if I leave you here." She shook her head. "My gut says go back. My heart can't say much because it's sort of in pieces." Navy met his eye with desperation in hers, almost a wild glint he'd never seen before.

He wanted to lean across the table and say, "Don't go."

He wanted to lean across the table and wipe her tears and say, "I love you. Don't go."

He wanted to lean across the table, take both of her hands in his and say, "I love you. Don't go back to Dallas. Let's get married and live at that ranch we looked at the other night."

He sat back in the booth, unsure of how to help her, what to say to her.

"Gavin," she said.

"You should do what you think is right." He would not be the one to persuade her one way or the other. If he did, and she ended up unhappy, she'd blame him forever.

*She's not Ginny*, he thought, but he still couldn't bring himself to ask her to stay with him.

The waitress arrived with Gavin's steak and Navy's chicken, leaving them alone again with the awkwardness between them. He picked at his baked potato, his appetite completely gone.

"Did you put an offer in on that ranch?" she asked, her voice normal now.

He noticed she wasn't eating either. "No," he said. "Busy day."

"But you're going to, right?"

Gavin exhaled and set his fork down. Every emotion he'd ever felt swirled inside him. "Why do you care, Navy?"

She blinked, a slight flinch at the fight in his tone. "It's your dream."

"Yeah, *mine*."

After a brief moment where she looked like she might cry again, she strengthened her shoulders and tossed her napkin onto the table. "Excuse me."

"Navy," he tried, but she stood and walked away from the table, never looking back. He couldn't help feeling like he'd just lost everything worth having in his life.

# Chapter Nineteen

Navy left the steakhouse despite Gavin's protests. She walked through the evening heat toward the fountain several blocks south. Each step radiated her anger. Anger at herself for not being able to make a decision. Anger at Gavin for not helping her. Anger at herself for telling him she loved him. Anger at Gavin that he hadn't repeated it back to her.

Left right, left right. Anger, anger. Anger, anger.

She arrived at the fountain in the middle of historic downtown and gazed up at the faces of the people carved into the statue. The fight left her muscles, leaving her with only indecision. She wasn't sure how to have everything she wanted. She'd worked in Dallas for years. She loved her job most of the time.

But she'd come to Three Rivers to change her life, and she'd met Gavin. Was she just supposed to throw that away? Her thoughts only brought agony, and she hated the helpless feelings plaguing her.

She dug in her purse and pulled out three shiny pennies. Rubbing her thumb along their smooth edges, she whispered, "Help me know what to do." She tossed all the coins into the wishing well at the same time.

Navy wasn't sure what she expected to happen. A voice from heaven? A ray of light that would form into an arrow and point her in the right direction?

The ripples in the fountain pulsed into stillness, and there was no voice. No light. No feeling.

Navy was lost, and she didn't know what to do. Gavin's words stung that his dreams were his, almost like he didn't want to share them with her. She'd shared all of hers with him. Told him all about her desires to be a mother, to have a stable family life with someone she loved.

*Don't give up on him*, she thought, and she wasn't sure if it was her brain giving the direction or not.

Almost immediately afterward, she thought, *You need to go back to Dallas.*

She sighed as she turned from the statue and the fountain. A giggly brunette practically skipped up the sidewalk to the statue, and she leaned her weight into both hands on the wall surrounding the fountain.

Laughing, she tilted her head toward the sky. "I made it. I finally made it."

Navy watched her for a moment, complete in her

happiness to be in Three Rivers, where she probably thought all her dreams would come true.

Bitterness coated her throat, and her salad threatened to make another appearance. Navy turned away from the woman, seeing her own immaturity in thinking a legend or a myth could bring her true love.

*But maybe it did.*

Navy didn't acknowledge the thought. She pulled out her phone and called Karen, her boss at the hospital. When she answered, Navy said, "I need three days to get back into town. Will that work?"

Karen squealed and then sighed, her relief and excitement evident in those two gestures. "Yes, can you come in on Sunday morning?"

Navy sighed. "Yes, but then I get a month of Sundays off."

"Deal. See you soon." Karen hung up, and Navy stood on Main Street in Three Rivers, realizing that while she hadn't made many friends here, she did love the town. A bus pulled out of the station—probably the vehicle that had delivered the bubbly brunette to town—filling the air with the scent of diesel fuel.

Navy glanced down the block to the steakhouse, where she imagined she could see Gavin sitting in his truck. Her heart felt like someone was trying to jam it into a narrow-necked bottle. She wanted to go back to the restaurant. Apologize. Kiss him and tell him she'd show up to their wedding, and she'd love to raise their family at Dripping Springs Ranch.

But her tongue thickened in her mouth, the words she wanted to say disappearing. She turned in the opposite direction. Her future wasn't in Three Rivers, Texas. And she knew it. So she stepped into the crosswalk and started toward the bus station. She bypassed it and eventually made it back to her cottage.

Almost instantly, Gavin texted. *You make it home?*

*Yes.* She pressed her phone to her chest, a flood of tears heating her face, trickling from her eyes. *I'm going back to Dallas tomorrow. I'm sorry, Gavin, but my future isn't here in Three Rivers.*

She wanted to say more, but she didn't know how. The words didn't come. So she left it at that, sent the message, and turned off her phone. Her movements after that came mechanically as she folded shirts and put them in her suitcase. She vacuumed, swept, mopped. She paused with her hand on the walls Gavin had reclaimed and beautified.

"Thank you for my time here," she whispered hours later when she finally fell into bed. "I wish I had more."

THE NEXT MORNING, Navy stepped up to the ticket window at the bus station. The light was still gray it was so early, but she knew the sun would rise in only thirty minutes, painting everything in glorious shades of gold, orange, and white. And the heat would come with it.

"Dallas," she said when it was her turn.

"That bus leaves in twenty minutes," the attendant said. "you better hurry."

Navy passed over her debit card, her pulse racing. "When's the next one?"

"Monday."

She couldn't stay here for four more days. Her thoughts would eat her up, and she wouldn't be able to stay away from Gavin, though that was clearly what he wanted. Room to live his own dreams. Room to think. Room without her in it.

With the ticket in her hand, she hurried as quickly as she could with her baggage to the loading area. The driver helped her stuff it in the little remaining space, and she got on the bus with her purse to find that nearly every seat had been taken. She managed to find one next to a man that smelled more like cologne than anything else. Flashing him a smile, her reality hit her.

Tears fell, and she sniffled loudly.

"You okay, darlin'?" the man asked. He was probably near her father's age and wore a similar style of cowboy hat to Gavin's.

"No," she said, fumbling through her purse for a tissue. The woman across the aisle handed her one, and Navy gratefully took it. "I came to Three Rivers to find a man, but—well, that's not true. I mean, it is." She buried her head in her hands, her words making no sense even to her.

"Tell us all about it," the woman said, and Navy didn't need any further encouragement. She started at the very beginning, with Aunt Izzie and Uncle Marvin.

By the time the bus approached Wichita Falls, where Gus and Bridgette were getting off, Navy had the attention of at least a dozen people. She'd told the whole story of her life over the past three months. One older woman kept dabbing her eyes, and Navy felt a special kinship for her as she'd claimed to have met her husband in Three Rivers many years ago. He'd since passed away.

"So, there it is." She heaved a deep breath. "I'm going back to Dallas, and he's buying a ranch."

Bridgette shook her head. "I don't know what to tell you."

"I do," Gus said. "You should figure out how to get back up to that ranch."

"It's not always that easy," Bridgette said with a sharp look in her eye.

"Oh, you," another woman said, swatting at Gus with a irate expression. "Don't listen to him. He doesn't have a romantic bone in his body."

"That's why you should listen to me," Gus said. "Don't listen to Lena. She never did get married." He added the last bit in a hushed voice that wasn't meant to be quiet.

Lena practically lunged over the top of the seat, her fist making solid contact with Gus's shoulder. He only laughed. "We're all headed to a family reunion," he explained. "Seems like I'm gettin' the fighting over before we even get there."

Navy settled back into her seat as the bus slowed and made turns through the city to the station. Activity happened as they pulled in as people collected their bags and trash.

"Don't worry, Navy," Bridgette said. "I believe God will put you where you should be."

Similar sentiments were given by the others who'd tuned into her sob story, and she even gave a few hugs to a few of the ladies before they exited the bus. With about half the people still on board, Navy settled into Gus's seat next to the window and leaned her forehead against the glass.

*You should figure out how to get back up to that ranch.* His words wouldn't leave her head. Which ranch? The one where Gavin worked now? Or the one he was going to buy?

And Bridgette had been right too. Things weren't always so black and white. So cut and dried.

Navy was so tired thinking about it. She closed her eyes and put in her headphones, hoping that loud music and the rhythmic movement of the bus would put her thoughts to bed.

* * *

LYNN MET her at the bus station with a wide smile and a huge hug. Navy held on tightly to her friend, grateful she'd left her own family in order to help Navy.

"Thank you," she said, the tears so close to the surface they spilled out again.

Lynn held her at arm's length, her eyes concerned and searching Navy's. "Oh, honey, you fell in love with him."

Navy didn't try to deny it. She nodded as a fresh flood of water washed down her cheeks. Nothing seemed like it would ever be right again. She wasn't sure how the sun was still shining or how people were walking down the streets of Dallas as if nothing had happened. Everything in Navy's world felt off-kilter.

"Come on," Lynn said from beside her. "This calls for pizza and ice cream. Roy's taken the kids to a movie, so I'm not expected to be home for hours."

Navy let her best friend navigate her to her car, let her order the cheesiest pizza and the biggest Diet Coke that Freddy's Pizza offered. Lynn talked through most of dinner, and Navy ate only because her friend was watching her with those hawk eyes. The crust tasted like cardboard, and the cheese seemed too gloppy to be as delicious as Navy usually found it.

"This is bad," Lynn said.

"It is bad," Navy said. "Someone said I should figure out how to get back to Dripping Springs, but—"

"Wait. Dripping Springs?"

"Yeah, Gavin's found a ranch named Dripping

Springs. It's not the town down in Hill Country. It's about an hour from Three Rivers. I think the closest town is called Springville."

A smile the size of the Grand Canyon filled Lynn's face. She sat back in her chair, her dark hair fluttering around her face. "Oh this is perfect."

"It is?"

"Didn't you text me that your future wasn't in Three Rivers?"

"Yeah," Navy said, reaching for the unappetizing pizza slice on her plate. She couldn't bring herself to put it in her mouth. "And it's not, Lynn. I *felt* it." She wished she hadn't. Wished God had directed her in a different way in that regard. But He seemed to be silent on everything else except for that.

"Well, that's all fine," Lynn said. "Because you're not going to be living in Three Rivers."

"No, I'm not." Navy put the pizza down and signaled the waiter to come over. He did, and she asked, "Do you have any salads?"

"Sure. Caesar, chopped vegetable with chicken, and Cobb."

"I'll take the chopped. No chicken though. With ranch dressing."

He nodded and left, and a bit of normality crept into Navy at the thought of eating her despair through a salad.

"No, you're not," Lynn said, that smile starting to annoy Navy. "Because you're going to be living in

*Springville.* With Gavin Redd, and if I may quote from one of your texts...." She lifted her phone as if she really was going to read from their text stream. "One of the hottest cowboys Texas has ever produced."

A giggle jumped from Navy's mouth. "I did not say that."

Lynn stared at the phone for an extra moment. "On July fifth, to be exact." She turned the phone for Navy to check.

Instead of looking at Lynn's screen, despair clouded her vision. "Do you really think I can go back? What would that even look like?"

"Do you love him or not?"

"Yes." Navy sighed.

"Then you go talk to Karen to take care of your job here. I mean, you might need to find something up there, and Karen could write you a great letter of recommendation. Don't burn any bridges, you know? Then you find out when he'll be at his ranch, and you get on up there and surprise him."

"Sure, surprise him." Navy leaned forward as the waiter set her salad in front of him. "So tell me how Finn is doing. Wasn't he going through a bit of depression?" With the topic of Lynn's fifteen-year-old on the table, Navy was able to turn the conversation away from her.

*Surprise him* floated through her mind even after Lynn dropped her off at her stale, empty apartment. At least she had somewhere to stay that wasn't filled with her mother's questions and her sister's perfection. She'd have to face them soon enough, but she wasn't looking forward to it.

All she could think was *surprise him*. How could she even do that?

# Chapter Twenty

Gavin stared after the bus as it went down the street. He'd been five minutes too late. Five blasted minutes. If only he hadn't stopped by Navy's cottage. He'd found it empty—and it was more than physically empty. Sure, there were still couches and all the dishes and the bed she'd slept in for three months.

But he'd known as soon as he'd opened the door that she was gone, because her spirit wasn't there. Gavin could feel the void everywhere, and he hated how things had ended with them. Him calling her name as she stomped out of the steakhouse, her salad only half gone. He'd never get that image out of his head.

Frustration frothed in his veins. He'd texted her several times. Called her twice. Without an answer, he'd had no choice but to hunt her down. The bus rounded the corner, and she was truly gone.

*Gone.*

He wiped his hand through his hair and put his cowboy hat back on properly. It had nearly fallen off in his haste to get to the loading area. He returned to his truck, where all three dogs waited for him, panting up a storm.

He took them to the bark park, where they ran and drank a lot of water. Where he stewed over what to do next. He wasn't sure how to keep functioning with this massive hole in his chest, but he'd done it before. He could do it again.

Couldn't he?

With the dogs loaded up, he drove slowly back toward his grandparents' house to drop them off. As he passed the Old Main Hill Bed & Breakfast, the wild thought to purchase it instead of the ranch swam through his mind.

But everything about the idea felt false. He even squirmed in his seat. "I should buy the ranch," he said aloud to himself. And that sat right in his gut, the same way his decision to stay in Three Rivers and take care of his grandparents had all those years ago.

He set the dogs to go about their business in the yard and hurried into his house to find the folder Stephanie-the-Realtor had given him. He dialed her, and opened with, "I want to buy Dripping Springs Ranch. What do I do next?"

She'd told him her future wasn't in Three Rivers, and he'd always known his wasn't either. He'd even texted that to her. He wondered if she'd read the message, deleted it sight unseen, blocked his number, or what.

Stephanie led him through the steps to get funding, and the next month brought new and unique challenges to Gavin as he tried to prove he could financially afford the five hundred acre ranch, as he dealt with his feelings for an absent Navy, as he had to arrange Grandmother's and Granddad's transition of care.

Aunt Ally wasn't set to arrive until the end of October, but Gavin was hoping to be long gone by then. He couldn't stand to see any more flirtatious women at The Stable, or lingering around the bark park after they'd come into town on the bus.

"Garage is done," he announced to Blue one afternoon in mid-September. He pulled the door down and latched it. "We have to clear out tomorrow, guys. The carpet cleaners are coming." Blue, Misfit, and Miles looked at him like he had abandoned them when Navy had left town. "Why the sad faces? I told you we're all goin' to this new ranch, Dripping Springs. Then we'll call Navy and see if she'll come too." He clapped his hands together to get some of the loose dust off them and crouched to scrub Blue's head and neck.

He hadn't enjoyed the talk with Squire about quitting, especially since Gavin had thought all his problems would be solved if he could just get a job at Three Rivers. But in the end, he'd secured his own ranch.

"And if she won't answer, we'll go up to Amarillo and find her," he added darkly.

"She won't answer."

Gavin turned to find Grandmother sitting in the shade on his front porch, a stone's throw from where he'd been talking to himself. They'd briefly discussed Navy's abrupt departure from Three Rivers, and Grandmother had cautioned him to give her a bit of time.

As he approached the porch, he wondered if six weeks was enough time. It felt like six decades to Gavin. "Why won't she answer?" he asked.

"She's still trying to figure herself out." Grandmother's needle went in and out of the fabric in her lap. "Once she does, she'll come find you."

"So I'm just supposed to wait until she comes?"

Grandmother shrugged, but with her shoulders so bowed and round, it was hard to tell.

Gavin exhaled as he sat in the chair beside her. "I don't want to wait."

Grandmother glanced up, a curious, far-away look on her face. "A waiting person is a patient person." She went back to her sewing as if she hadn't spoken at all. A moment later, she looked at Gavin as if she hadn't seen him sit down. "Oh, Granddad is making ribs for dinner. He's over there dry rubbing right now." She chuckled as if the thought of Granddad massaging spices into pork was funny.

Gavin gawked at her. Was this how her matchmaking

sessions went? No wonder the women who came out of her studio didn't have their thoughts straight. "So I'll come for dinner," Gavin said. "But tomorrow, I'm going over to Dripping Springs to sign all the papers, remember?"

"We remember." Grandmother stood, her time on his porch obviously over. Gavin wasn't sure he'd ever seen her over here. It was more Granddad's style to sit on Gavin's front porch and talk.

She ambled away, and a pinch of guilt doused Gavin. But he wasn't moving until the end of the month, and they'd only be here for three weeks without help. Still, he knew they'd miss him terribly, and he'd miss them.

"It's only a seventy-minute drive," he told himself. He could make that in an evening, or every Sunday if he wanted to.

The following day, he loaded the dogs and his granddad into the truck for the journey to Dripping Springs Ranch. His stomach fluttered like he'd swallowed birds for breakfast, when the reality was he hadn't eaten at all. Sleep had eluded him as well. Somehow purchasing this ranch seemed like the very biggest thing he'd ever done in his life, and he didn't want anything to go wrong.

So when he blew a tire thirty minutes outside of Springville, he very nearly lost his mind. The morning sun in Texas was only slightly kinder than the afternoon, and Gavin managed to get the spare on without breaking anything.

Granddad seemed worse for the wear, so Gavin pulled

off at the next gas station for something to drink. "You okay, Granddad?" Gavin peered at the man he loved most, his heart clenching a bit too tight.

"Fine, fine." But Granddad always said that, and his legs wobbled the slightest bit as he got out of the truck again. "I would like a sweet tea."

Gavin made him sit in a display chair just inside the convenience store while he went in search of drinks. He also grabbed some beef jerky and potato chips, both of which Granddad loved and that would give him some extra salt.

When they were finally back on the road, headed in the right direction, at the right speed, Granddad ripped open the chips and said, "I'm gonna miss you, Gavin," followed by the crunch of the sour cream and cheddar potato chips.

His simple words unlocked the floodgate Gavin had put on his emotions the morning he'd watched that bus drive away. A shudder shook his chest, and he cleared his throat to keep the sob inside.

"I know, Granddad." He reached across the distance between them and squeeze his grandfather's hand. "I know. I'm gonna miss you too."

Several minutes later, he pulled into Springville and started talking. Detailing the quaint little town was better than thinking, and it got him through until the turn out to the ranch. "See? It's not that far. I bet I'll come home every weekend."

"Three Rivers never was your home," Granddad said, stalling Gavin's pulse for a moment.

"What do you mean?"

"You've never been happy there. You stayed because we needed you, and we're so grateful. But we knew you'd need to leave eventually." Granddad exhaled and brushed snack crumbs from his fingers. "I'm surprised you've stayed as long as you have."

Gavin didn't know what to say. He'd reassured his grandparents many times over the years that he wanted to be in Three Rivers, wanted to be right where he was. Even as he'd said it, he now realized that his fantasies had always taken him from the town, away into the wilds of Texas.

"Granddad? What does Grandmother tell the women who come to see her?" Gavin tried not to look at him, but it was altogether impossible.

"Oh, let's see." Granddad smiled and let out a long sigh, one that went on and on like he'd been holding it inside for a while. "She doesn't tell me much, you see. But she does say a few things. Mostly she just wants those girls to be happy, and that the one that's standin' in their way is usually them."

Gavin's jaw tightened. "So she doesn't tell them they have to marry an Aquarius or whatever."

"She probably mentions some stuff like that. Compatibility charts and the like. Chinese New Year animals were big one year in the eighties."

Gavin blinked, sure he'd heard wrong. A burst of laughter came from his mouth. "So it *is* all bunk."

"No, of course not," Granddad said with increased passion in his voice. "What Grandmother does is serious. She does tell them who they'd be most compatible with. What they do with the information is up to them."

"She told Navy she needed to be with an Aquarius. Only luck played into that one for me." He pulled up to the title company and put the truck in park. He searched his granddad's face. "I love her, Grandad, but what if I hadn't been an Aquarius?"

A sparkle entered his weathered face, brightening his eyes back to that deep-lake blue that Gavin had always cherished. "I think she would've still fallen in love with you."

"She left."

"She'll come back."

Gavin tilted his head, grasping for some of his granddad's confidence. "How do you know?"

"She's one of the good ones. That's what your grandmother said after Navy's reading. Did you know that? Came right upstairs and said, 'She's one of the good ones. I hope she learns what she needs to about herself and gets out of her own way.'" He reached over and patted Gavin's shoulder. "Then she sighed like she does when she really wants to help someone and doesn't know how."

"Hmm." Gavin didn't know what else to say. And he

had a ranch to buy. "Let's go," he said. "I think you'll like watching me sign papers for the next three hours."

Grandad half-wheezed and half-chuckled, and together they made their way into the office, where a mountain of paperwork waited.

* * *

A WEEK LATER, Gavin stood in the homestead on the ranch, the key to the front door still in his hand. Happiness flooded him, rushing and gushing through his whole body. He hadn't felt this alive since the first time he'd kissed Navy.

*Navy.*

Her name made his heart ache, and a sound like a gong reverberating sang through his eardrums. He'd put off calling her all these weeks, but he couldn't wait any longer. He dialed her number, praying with the strength of the sun, the moon, and the stars that she wouldn't be at work, or sleeping, or ignoring him still.

Her voicemail picked up, sending disappointment through his lingering joy. He almost hung up, but something pricked him to stay on the line. "Navy," he said. "It's Gavin Redd. You know, the man who loves you up in Three Rivers? Well, I'm not in Three Rivers anymore, and you said in your last text to me that your future wasn't there. I'm wondering if you think it might be in Springville, on a little ranch called Dripping Springs." He exhaled and looked at the yellow walls he was about to paint gray. "Anyway, give me a call back when you get this."

He wasn't sure if he should end with "I love you," Or "Goodbye," or what, so he just hung up. Then he did what Gavin did best when he felt his life slipping out of control.

He worked.

# Chapter Twenty-One

"Come in, come in." Aunt Izzie gestured to Navy from halfway in the house, her wrinkled hand flapping in the fierce wind that had descended on Texas Hill Country.

Navy hurried inside just before it started raining. The microburst would only last for a few minutes, but she didn't want to be caught outside when it hit. No one did.

"Hey, Aunt Izzie." Navy embraced her great aunt who bore a smile and the scent of peaches. Oh, how Navy loved that scent. It reminded her so much of love, as Aunt Izzie had never shown her anything but acceptance. "Thanks for the invitation to dinner."

"Pish posh," Aunt Izzie said, bustling into the kitchen where Uncle Marvin kept watch over a pot on the stove. "Your mother tells me you haven't been home to see them yet."

"I call her all the time."

"I'm sure you do." Aunt Izzie picked up a knife, and Navy thought her great aunt would lose a fingertip by the end of the evening. But she managed to get the knife through a red bell pepper and then a yellow one.

"You're avoiding them," Aunt Izzie said without a trace of questioning in her tone. "Your mother knows it."

"Maybe she'll explode with her questions before I make it over there." Navy collapsed onto a barstool and frowned. "I just don't want to go see Lexie all joyful-joyful with my ex-boyfriend. I don't understand why everyone doesn't get that."

"I get it," Aunt Izzie said.

"You always do." Navy smiled for a brief moment, the connection between her and her aunt as strong as ever. "I met someone in Three Rivers."

"I know you did."

"You do?"

"He's called me four times, looking for you. Gavin Redd? Did you know he stays with us every year when he calls the auction?"

"I do now." Navy twirled a piece of her hair around her fingers. "He's called?"

"He says he's called you too." Aunt Izzie gave her a sharp look and went back to her chopping.

Navy rested her chin in her palm. "I've only been home a week. I don't know what to do."

"Maybe put the poor man out of his misery."

Uncle Marvin turned from the stove. "These are done, dear." He beamed a smile in Navy's direction and set about draining the rice noodles as if he was deaf to the conversation around him.

"I thought I was," Navy said as Aunt Izzie set a cast iron skillet on the stove and jacked the flame to high underneath it. The peppers and onions went in, and moments later, so did a bowlful of marinating chicken. Aunt Izzie stir fried while the hot, snapping, sizzling sounds filled the kitchen. The scent of meat being browned and turned into something delicious rose into the air, along with the distinct smell of teriyaki and pineapple.

Moments later, the drained rice noodles went in with the meat, and Aunt Izzie stirred stirred stirred before transferring the pot to the counter right in front of Navy. "Dinner's ready."

Navy made it through the meal, grateful she hadn't had to go through another Sunday evening alone. She'd gotten used to eating with Gavin and his grandparents on Sundays after church, and she'd never felt as alone as she had last weekend after her shift.

She lingered on her great aunt's couch with a cup of coffee, not wanting to return to her apartment, where even her cat had chosen to ignore her.

Gavin had called, but Navy hadn't been brave enough to answer. In Three Rivers, she was always the one to turn the other cheek, ask him to go to lunch when she wanted him to invite her. Insist he take her to the steakhouse when she really only wanted to eat French fries and salad.

"How's work?" Uncle Marvin asked, and Navy pulled herself from her dismal thoughts.

"Great," she said as brightly as she could muster. "We had a mother come in yesterday afternoon, pretty far along already. She didn't have any time to get her shots or anything, and I coached her through the birth." Navy's chest warmed at the memory of joy on that mother's face. "She had a baby girl."

"What did she name her?" Aunt Izzie asked absently.

Navy paused as she took in how Aunt Izzie and Uncle Marvin sat beside each other on the loveseat. Their hands were intertwined, and he seemed to know exactly when she wanted her coffee because he took it from the end table and extended it to her without Aunt Izzie requesting it.

Navy suddenly wanted to leave. Maybe being alone in her apartment with her prissy cat was better than watching two people so in love. Wasn't that what she was avoiding by not going home? She couldn't bear the thought of being face-to-face with Lexie and Scott. Or John and his fiancée Ashley. She couldn't tell them she'd left Gavin in Three Rivers, just to come home and work at the hospital again.

A sour feeling crept up her throat, and no matter how much coffee she gulped to tame it, the emotion kept climbing. She spun the ring on her thumb, then her pointer finger, but her feelings would not be deterred. Before they could infect her vocal chords, she stood. "Thanks for everything, Aunt Izzie," she said, her voice only straying higher on the last word. "But I have to run." She put her coffee mug in the sink and skated kisses across both of their foreheads.

She'd just made it outside when the first band of pressure attached itself to her chest. By the time she got home, she could barely breathe.

* * *

Weeks passed, and Navy was no closer to finding a solution to her heart problems. Unfortunately, the cardiologists at the hospital didn't know what to do about a broken heart either.

And so Navy suffered through her shifts. Through lunches with her friends. Through lonely evenings. Through church on Sundays. She put on a brave face, the one she'd worn after her break-up with Scott, which had really taken her out of the dating game for a year or two. When she had to, she put on a smiling face. Or a concerned face.

But she was simply passing time. Getting through every day. Breathing in and out without really living.

By the time October rolled around, Gavin hadn't made contact in weeks. It seemed like he'd given up after the first few days, and Navy felt more alone and abandoned than ever.

"Which is completely ridiculous," she told herself as she went down to get the x-rays for a newborn that had come into the world prematurely. Her voice echoed around the stairwell as she continued, "You're the one who left him. *You* abandoned *him*."

And all at once, Navy knew why she hadn't been able to answer his calls or read his texts. Her embarrassment and humiliation simply wouldn't let her. She practically punched open the door leading back into the hospital, and her fingers shot pain into her elbow and up her arm.

She collected the x-rays the doctor needed and instead of taking the elevator back up to Labor & Delivery where the mother waited, she opted for the stairs again. Her chest burned with the effort of climbing five very tall floors, but she felt more in control of herself by the time she returned.

She knocked quietly and entered the room, unsure of what she'd find inside. The mom cradled her baby against her chest, with the father standing watch near her head. Two elderly people—clearly grandparents—waited nervously by the window.

The doctor was talking, and Navy caught the end of what he said. "...what it is, we'll know. And we'll be able to do something. You just need to be brave, and let us deal with it." He turned toward Navy. "Ah, here are our x-rays now." Dr. Candelis smiled at Navy, but she'd worked with him enough to see the underlying tension in the lines around his mouth.

She handed him the x-rays and he put them on the light box on the wall. Navy focused on her job, but it was really hard with *be brave, be brave, be brave* bouncing around inside her brain.

Hours later, after she'd worked a double shift and felt like she'd been run over by a tractor, she finally left work. Her phone flashed red, blue, and green lights at her, but she couldn't bear to open it and see all the messages. Probably more guilt-ridden texts from her mom about working too much, not coming over, blah blah *blah*.

Navy drove through a pizza place that had pepperoni and cheese pizzas waiting in the warmer and headed home. For once, Apricot her orange tabby cat, stayed in the living room after Navy had entered. For once, Navy didn't change before digging into her dinner. For once, she didn't care about any of it.

She stood over the sink, eating through three slices of pepperoni and cheese before she felt human again. The darkness outside her window testified that fall was coming, and she better get on board with an earlier sunset.

After kicking off her shoes, she laid down on the couch and faced her phone. Four Facebook messages, seven texts, and three missed calls. She started with the calls, and her heart practically choked her when she saw Gavin's name. Not only that, but he'd left a message.

"Navy."

Every muscle in her body spasmed at the bass sound of her name in his voice.

"It's Gavin Redd. You know, the man who loves you up in Three Rivers? Well, I'm not in Three Rivers anymore, and you said in your last text to me that your future wasn't there. I'm wondering if you think it might be in Springville, on a little ranch called Dripping Springs." He exhaled and she could just picture him standing on the ranch, that hopeful look in his eyes as he spoke. "Anyway, give me a call back when you get this."

The message ended, and Navy stared at the phone as the electronic voicemail maiden gave her options. She stabbed the five with her pointer to hear the message again. And then again.

She missed him so much. Forgotten the sound of his voice. The touch of his hand in hers. The taste of his mouth.

Before she could think, or get up and drown her problems in more pizza, she hit the button to return the message sender's call.

# Chapter Twenty-Two

Gavin woke to the shrill peal of his phone ringing. In his disorientation, he hit it off the arm of the couch. It hit the floor with a heart-stopping crack and skittered off somewhere, going silent in the process.

He sat straight up, trying to figure out where he was. Several seconds passed before he recognized the shape of the room, the front door before him, the tall lamps standing sentinel in the corners.

"The ranch." He breathed out a sigh of relief, the adrenaline that had him on fight mode leaking away. But he'd still misplaced his phone and missed a call.

His muscles screamed as he got up. Though he'd spent days painting before, these walls had sucked at the new color like camels that hadn't had a drink in years. He'd worked well past the point of comfort, all in an attempt to keep his mind from rotating around a certain blonde woman he couldn't stop thinking about.

Hope buoyed his spirits as he hunted for the light switch. Maybe Navy had returned his call. Since he'd been in Springville, only one person had called—Steve. Gavin initiated all the calls to his grandparents, and they seemed genuinely happy to hear from him every other day.

He found the phone halfway under the entertainment center he'd assembled and then left in the middle of the room so he could paint. He didn't have a TV yet, but he'd ordered one online and it should be arriving in the next few days.

He found his phone and flipped it over. The screen was playing tricks on him. It said Navy had called.

The adrenaline came back twice as strong now, and he nearly dropped the phone again as his hands turned slick. His head felt detached from his body as he hadn't eaten dinner yet. He stumbled into the kitchen and turned on the sink.

Splashing water on his face gave him the needed mental edge, and he pulled open the refrigerator though he'd been going to town each day for food. Thankfully, he had a box containing half of his burrito from lunch.

He eyed his phone while he waited for the microwave to heat up his dinner. He couldn't believe Navy had called him back. As the food went round and round to the whir of the machine, Gavin realized he'd given up hope.

And he hated that. He hated that he'd allowed himself to fall so deep and then stay down there in the pit of despair.

"She called back," he whispered to the mostly dark house. The microwave beeped, and he pulled his food out. With every bite, all he could think was *she called back. She called back.*

Satisfied that he would be able to listen to her and have an intelligent, non-emotional conversation, he threw the now-empty container in the trash can and touched the button to return Navy's call.

She answered on the second ring, her "Hello?" like music to his very soul.

"Navy." His voice broke. So much for non-emotional.

"Gavin." She sounded as broken as he felt.

He cleared his throat and focused on a cobweb above the fridge. "Did you listen to my message?"

"Yes."

"What do you think? Springville isn't Three Rivers."

"I can't get there on a bus. I already looked."

The room spun. "So you'll come?"

"I can't come right away. You realize that, right? I have to do things right."

Gavin nodded though they weren't in the same physical space. "I don't know what any of that means. What do you need to do right?"

"Quit my job so I can get another one up there. Get a

good letter of recommendation from my boss. Find someone to take my lease. That kind of stuff."

His mouth felt sticky and sandy at the same time. "Oh, right. Do you need any help?"

She sighed in that exasperated way of hers, but her voice was kind when she said, "I just need time."

"Navy, I've got nothing but time." He grinned, his imagination running wild. The very thought of Navy living with him on this ranch...he could barely contain his excitement. His joy. His gratitude.

"So maybe you'll call me again tomorrow?" she asked, and he could just see that devilish, flirtatious glint in her eye. The upturned corners of her beautiful mouth.

"Maybe," he teased.

She laughed, and the ice that lingered between them shattered under the sound of it. "I've missed you," she said between chuckles.

That sobered him, and he said, "I miss you every day. So much it hurts."

"I know. I'm sorry I—"

"Navy, let's wait until we're together to do all that," he said.

"Why?"

"Because I don't want to hear you say I'm sorry. I want to hold you while you say it. Kiss the words away. Help you know that I'm fine, and we'll make this work. And I can't do that over the phone." He inhaled. "So, tell me about work. Anything exciting going on?"

"Actually, there was a mother who delivered today that helped me be brave enough to call you back...."

*** * ***

GAVIN PARKED at the bark park, but he didn't have his dogs with him. He had a fresh haircut, a ton of time invested in something he hoped Navy would like, and a gut full of angry bees.

He strolled over to the fountain where people threw in coins and made wishes like he was Mr. Cool. At this time of night, there wasn't anyone else around, and that suited Gavin just fine. After all, he needed to have a little talk with a fountain.

Gazing up at the statue there, he exhaled. "You've sure made my life difficult."

The water continued to bubble, not really caring that women came here to throw in coins, make husband wishes, and then go see the matchmaker.

"But I forgive you," Gavin said. A breeze kicked up, stealing his words and causing him to wish he'd brought a jacket on this Halloween evening. He'd eaten more than his fair share of cupcakes at the park, and he'd even helped pass out candy to the kids as they made the rounds. Halloween signaled the end of the summer dances, something Gavin had never really attended but which drew a large crowd on weekend nights.

But now he was just waiting. Waiting for a bus from Dallas. Waiting for the woman of his dreams.

"It would be nice if you could make sure things work out this time." He wasn't sure if he was talking to himself, to the fountain, or to God.

A tingle started on the back of his neck, a feeling of being watched. He turned toward Main Street behind him, but there was no one there. Still, he thought there was something...different in the air now.

He waited, standing and watching. And waited, now sitting on a bench at the entrance of the bark park. And waited, perched on the edge of the fountain closest to the bus station.

Finally, the big beast pulled into town, bringing its loud engine and scent of burnt rubber. He stood, sliding his palms down the front of his thighs, trying not to let his anxiety get the better of him.

He failed completely when the brakes hissed, and the bus lowered. His boots carried him toward the street, his heart pounding in time to his steps. He'd just rounded the front of the bus when the doors clanked open, and the first person got off.

It wasn't Navy.

Two more passengers disembarked and moved alongside the bus to get their luggage before Gavin saw her.

His breath caught.

She was more beautiful than ever, though she'd been riding on a bus for ten hours. Navy clutched something in her fist and her smile seemed to light up the whole state of Texas.

Her feet landed on the pavement, and she stalled for exactly one pulse of his heart. Then she rushed him, her laughter soaring into the sky with his. He received her willingly, swept her off her feet and around in a circle, trying very hard to commit every touch, every breath of her floral skin, every beat of her laughter to his memory.

"I love you," he said, setting her on her feet. He cradled her face in both of his hands. "I love you, Navy Richards."

She reached up and bumped his already skewed cowboy hat. It fell off, and she caught it before it hit the ground. With her free hand, she tiptoed her fingers up his chest and slid them along the side of his face.

Fire erupted in his core, boiling out and up and over. "I love you too, Gavin Redd."

He grinned, whooped, and kissed her. This kiss was very much like the first. Life-changing. Passionate. And Gavin knew he'd never kiss anyone but her again.

Someone beyond them started clapping, and Gavin pulled away, still grinning.

The bus driver stood near the doors, a wide smile on his face. "I see now why y'all needed your ticket to Three Rivers."

Navy held up what she'd been clutching in her hand. "Thanks, Dennis."

"You go on, now," he said in a thick Southern accent. "Y'all gonna marry that man."

Navy glanced at Gavin, a sheepish look on her face. "Dennis, shh. I haven't asked him yet."

The man threw a boisterous laugh into the sky before saying, "I think he'll agree," and getting back on the bus.

Gavin gaped at him. "Who's that?"

"Oh, my new best friend," Navy said. She went to retrieve her suitcase, and Gavin helped get her big one, shooting her a squinty-eyed look. "What? It's a ten-hour bus ride. I had to talk to someone."

He shook his head and chuckled. "Well, come on. I have something to show you before the night is up."

He led her across the street to the fountain, and her steps slowed the closer they went. "Come on," he said. "It doesn't bite."

Navy approached slowly, a dubious expression on her face. He reached out and fingered her hair, glad he could. Beyond glad. He swept his lips against her temple, and skated them down the side of her face to her ear.

She giggled and wrapped herself in his embrace. "I thought you didn't like this fountain."

"Oh, I really don't," Gavin said. "But we've sort of come to an understanding." He fished in his jeans pocket for a moment and produced two gold Sacagawea dollar coins. "But I thought maybe we could each make a wish."

"Wow, we've got a high roller here." She glanced around as if a crowd had followed them. When she discovered they were alone, she turned back to him. "You sure about this?"

"I've had my wish ready since you called a month ago." He flipped his coin over and over again. "Have you got one?"

She thought for a few moments, and then a smile spread her lips. "Yeah, I'm ready."

*"On one, two, three."* He flipped his coin into the *wishing well with the thought,* Wish I may, wish I might, have this wish I wish tonight: I wish for Navy to be my wife.

He opened his eyes and looked into Navy's. A shy smile stole across her features, and he tucked her hand in his. "Let's go."

Gavin drove slowly through town, telling her how nothing had changed since she'd left. Little in Three Rivers ever did, which was why the news of a runaway horse and how he'd saved her had practically catapulted him into stardom.

When he didn't get on the main highway so they could make the drive to Springville, she perked up.

"Where are we going?"

"I said I had something to show you."

"I thought that was the fountain."

He scoffed. "No, this is something much better."

Her head went back and forth like she was watching a very interesting tennis match as he drove. He finally pulled into the driveway of his old house. His aunt's car sat in the garage, and a few lights winked in the windows.

"I helped my aunt move in a few days ago," he said as he opened his door. He turned back to help Navy scoot out. His hands found her waist, and he couldn't help himself as he bent down and kissed her again. She tasted like chocolate and apples and something else he couldn't name.

She finally pushed vainly on his chest to get him to stop, and he pulled back. "Mm, it's so good to see you."

"It's a little late to visit your grandparents."

He faced the street. "We're not visiting them." He stepped toward the bed and breakfast on the other side of the road. "We're goin' over there."

Navy went with him for a few strides, and then paused when they hit the street. Outside of the lights, darkness quickly consumed everything. "Are you sure?" she asked. "Did someone buy it?"

"No."

"And we're going over there? Isn't that trespassing?"

He gave a light laugh, but the hair on the back of his neck stood up. "Look who's worried about trespassing now." He gently tugged on her hand to get her moving again.

"It's creepy in the dark," she said. "And I don't remember the ground being all that even."

"We're not going far."

"How far?"

"Just to the second cabin. The one you liked, remember?" He rounded the first cabin with the star on the front, and the lights he'd set up on the Texas Romance Cabin twinkled through the blackness.

Navy's breath caught in a sexy little gasp that made Gavin's pulse pound. "Gavin, what have you done?"

"It's nothing," he said. "But there's a little surprise inside."

She went with him, and he was grateful it was easier to see with the tea lights and candles he'd put inside and outside the cabin. He stepped in front of her to open the door, and he backed into the cabin so he could witness her reaction.

He'd covered the counter and table with candles and lights. In the center of the table sat a lava cake display with a dozen red roses, one on top of each cake.

"Lava cakes," he said. "I think we both like those."

Navy pressed one hand to her chest, right over her heart.

Gavin swept his hand toward the kitchen, where a tower of chocolate baklava sat. Her eyes widened. "Is that what I think it is?"

"Sure is, sweetheart."

She gazed up at him with such love, such adoration, in her expression, Gavin's bones turned to marshmallow. He hoped he could make her this happy every day for the rest of her life.

"I love chocolate baklava."

"I happen to know that." He beamed at her. "But what about this?" He bent and pulled a cooler around the side of the cabinet. With a flourish, he opened it to reveal more Diet Coke than had ever been seen in Three Rivers before.

A sob erupted from Navy's mouth at the same time she tried to laugh. The resulting noise sounded like the way Blue barked. He lifted his eyebrows and hoped he hadn't gone too far.

"You are something else," she said, reaching for a bottle of her favorite beverage.

"I have one more thing." Gavin went all the way into the kitchen and opened the drawer where he'd placed the little black box.

He came around again to stand in front of her. "I know you already have a kazillion rings. One for every finger, for every day of the week." He dropped to one knee and flipped open the box at the same time, a move he'd been practicing for weeks.

"Gavin, no," Navy breathed.

"Navy Richards, will you marry me?"

# Chapter Twenty-Three

Navy still had so many things she wanted to talk with Gavin about. But she immediately slipped the silver band off her left ring finger to make room for the engagement ring and said, "Yes," accompanied by a girlish giggle. She couldn't believe this was happening to her. Her, Navy, the woman who hadn't been on two dates in a row with the same guy until she'd met Gavin.

He slid the gold ring bearing a giant diamond on her finger, a slight tremor in his. She flung her arms around his neck and enjoyed the rush of affection flowing through her. "I can't believe we're going to get married."

"We can go down to Dallas, if that's what you want," he whispered just before nipping her earlobe between his teeth.

She laughed and tipped her head back. "Do I have to decide right now?"

"Nope."

"Good, because maybe I'd like to have the wedding in the park, right by that fountain." She watched him, hoping he'd hear the playfulness in her voice.

He clearly didn't, because he scowled and removed his hands from her waist. She jumped back into his arms. "It was a joke, Gavin."

The annoyance melted off his face, and he rolled his eyes. "I remember you being funnier."

"Hey." She swatted his chest and tried to escape from the circle of his arms. He held her fast, close, tight.

"Maybe your family would come to the ranch," he said in that gorgeous voice of his. "There's a nice preacher over there. Says good things."

"You think he'd do an on-site wedding?"

"Can't hurt to ask." Gavin threaded all ten of his fingers through hers and rocked back on his heels. "So, you wanna go?"

Navy drew in a deep breath and checked her back pocket for her ticket to Three Rivers. "Yeah." She smiled. As much as she loved this town, she didn't want to stay here. "Yeah, let's go to Springville."

He laughed. "We can't just go," he said. "We have to eat all this baklava and all those lava cakes...."

Navy glanced around at the elaborate setup Gavin had put together for her proposal. Her heart swelled with love, and she stepped toward the chocolate baklava and took a piece. One bite, and she moaned. "I love this stuff."

Gavin texted someone, and a few minutes later his grandparents and who Navy assumed was his Aunt Ally showed up. Several minutes after that, his friend Steve and his wife Carol arrived. The cooler of Diet Coke got carried to Gavin's truck. Everyone had some treats and Gavin's grandmother boxed up the leftovers.

Congratulations were issued, and candles blown out, and tea lights taken down. "You two go on," his aunt said. "I've got this."

"Aunt Ally bought the B-and-B," Gavin said. "She's going to fix it up and run it."

"Wow." Navy grinned at the brunette who had the same high forehead as Gavin and his grandfather. "That's great. I wanted Gavin to buy it."

"The ranch is much better," he said.

"I'm sure it is." Navy swung their hands between them. "Have you done any changes with it?"

"Nope. Well, I painted one of the barns a deeper red. And I've done some work inside the homestead." He tipped his head at his aunt and took Navy back outside.

"I can't wait to see it," she said.

"I can't wait to have you there." He tucked her against his side and brushed his lips against her temple.

A glow like the rising sun started inside Navy, and she basked in the golden warmth of it. And she finally knew what it felt like to be loved by a man that she also loved.

Two hours later, she curled into Gavin's side on the top step of his front porch. She'd fallen asleep almost instantly on the drive from Three Rivers to Springville, even though it was less than an hour away, so they hadn't had a chance to talk about anything.

And she didn't want to start now either. Her heart just felt so...blocked up, and she didn't want to ruin their reunion with needless talk. He didn't say much either, but he yawned about three times before she clued in to his exhaustion.

She jumped to her feet. "So we'll talk in the morning." She held out her hand for his keys. They'd agreed she'd take his truck that night to a hotel in town. He'd scoured the town for a place for her to stay, but she wanted to choose a place. "And we're going to look at those four houses, right?"

Gavin stood too, his gaze intense and diving right into her soul. "Right. You can come out anytime. I have chores here until about nine or ten at least."

"All right." Navy stretched up and pressed her lips to Gavin's, thrilled at the gentle way he stroked his fingers down the side of her face as he deepened the kiss. Navy ducked her head before she got too carried away. "I'm sorry, Gavin."

"We're fine, Navy."

She looked right into his eyes, and found the peace there. The joy. The love. She nodded, wishing she could forgive herself as easily as he seemed to have forgiven her. "I'll see you in the morning."

* * *

"Look," she said, leaning into the doorway of the barn where he worked. He glanced over his shoulder, a smile forming on his face.

She folded her arms. "I didn't leave you and Three Rivers for my job."

He approached as she spoke, his grin fading the closer he came. "I never thought that."

"I did." She frowned up at him. "Why did you think I left?"

He sighed. "Because you weren't sure I was your match. You didn't see a future for yourself in Three Rivers. That kind of thing."

She gawked at him. "I told you to your face that I loved you."

"It's easy to forget when a person calls and texts and only gets silence." He shuffled back a few steps and resumed his feeding of the horses.

Familiar shame darted through her. "I...I couldn't answer. I was embarrassed."

"Of what?"

"Of disappearing without giving you a chance to explain."

"What changed your mind?"

"I told you about the mother who had a baby with the arm deformities."

"Ah, yes. She had to be brave."

223

"Right."

"So why *did* you leave?"

Navy swallowed her fear now, the way she wished she had months ago. "I was afraid," she said. "I loved you, but I was being torn in several directions, and Dallas was the easiest one to go in." She shrugged against the doorframe, hoping her explanation would be good enough for him.

"All right." He barely looked at her as he finished up with the last horse. He dusted his hands together. "So let's go find you somewhere to live."

* * *

Navy finally made it to church several days after she'd settled into her new lodgings on the outskirts of Three Rivers. Gavin had helped her brighten up the walls, hang curtains, and tame the weeds that had taken over the lawn. She'd contracted a trucking company to get her furniture up here, and it had just arrived yesterday.

So she and Gavin had spent the morning getting the heavier items in the right rooms, and then he'd gone back to the ranch. He worked, and worked, and worked. Navy had managed to put in her application at the hospital in Three Rivers, and she'd go to the emergency center and doctor's offices if she had to.

"You ready?"

She glanced away from the gold-brick building that had a cross inlaid on the side. There were a surprising number of churches in Springville, and they'd passed several before Gavin had pulled into this one.

"Yes." She flashed him a smile and followed him out of his truck. "What's the pastor's name again?"

"Pastor Nye. He's fun. He laughs really loud. I think you'll like him." Gavin led her into the church and gestured her into a row near the back. Several pairs of eyes landed on her and stayed, checking her out. She wondered how many of them had befriended Gavin; he didn't seem to get off the ranch much.

A few people spoke to him, and he murmured hellos back to them. He didn't introduce her to anyone, and no one asked. Maybe they already knew about her. Maybe Springville didn't have nearly the gossip circles of other small Texas towns.

The choir started singing, startling Navy. She'd never heard such a rousing rendition of the hymn, and she was even more surprised when the people wearing royal blue robes parted, and out came a tall African-American man wearing the same robes and clapping for all he was worth.

He wore a giant smile and he went all the way to the pulpit before turning back to the choir. He waved his hands left and right and then cut them off. They silenced instantly, and the man turned around.

"Brothers and sisters!" he bellowed into the mic. "Isn't it a great day to be alive?"

"Isn't he great?" Gavin asked, leaning over.

Two seconds passed while Navy's mind whirred. "*He's* the pastor?"

"Now you know why we passed all those other churches." Gavin settled his arm around her as Pastor Nye began his enthusiastic sermon on forgiveness. Navy groaned inwardly; the last thing she wanted was a lecture on forgiveness.

But Gavin was right; everything Pastor Nye said made her want to hear what he said next, and she couldn't look away from his animated face.

"Have you taken your problems to the Lord?" he asked. "He has already borne all our griefs. He has already been wronged the way you have. Why carry that burden?"

Navy found herself nodding and adding a whispered "Amen," when the rest of the congregation did. Gavin said nothing but he maintained his focus on the man at the front of the chapel.

"And not only that, my friends, but we must examine ourselves too. Do we have things we need to be forgiven of? People we can beg for that forgiveness. I say to you today: Don't delay. Go to them. Apologize. Set things right." He scanned the congregation, his mood sobering the slightest bit. The power and fire in his eyes did not, and Navy felt his words all the way down in her toes when he said, "And the hardest type of forgiveness of all—that of forgiving one's self."

Navy stiffened and Gavin's fingers curled around her shoulder protectively.

"We all do things we regret," he said. "Even when it seems the other party has forgiven us, we may struggle to let go of our own shortcomings. Don't do that to yourself." He shook his head and smacked his lips together. "Just don't. I know how hard it can be to let go. It requires faith and trust in the Lord Jesus Christ. Go to Him. He will help you find your way to forgiveness."

He stepped back from the microphone then, grinned for all he was worth, and turned back to the choir. Navy found herself—and everyone else in the chapel—smiling too. The choir launched into another hymn that seemed a bit too loud and raucous to belong in a church, but Navy still felt a peaceful power coursing through her.

She wanted to forgive herself for leaving Three Rivers the way she had. She'd apologized to Gavin. He'd obviously forgiven her. Now she just needed to figure out how to give away the burden currently weighing down her entire frame.

# Chapter Twenty-Four

Gavin watched Navy struggle with her inadequacies for a week. Then two. Just before their third Sunday of attending church together, she bounded out of her two-bedroom house on the east edge of Three Rivers, a big smile on her face. Her deep plum dress billowed behind her and he couldn't get out of the truck fast enough to receive her.

She yanked open the passenger door and climbed in, scooting over to place a kiss on his cheek. "Guess what?"

He could answer in any number of ways, but he chose to simply go with, "What?"

"I got a job."

Joy lifted his spirits. "That's great, sweetheart. Where?"

"The hospital finally decided I was the one they wanted."

He knew she'd interviewed several times, and that they'd narrowed the candidates down to two and then kept them waiting for a week. He laughed and leaned over to kiss her properly. "That's great. We should celebrate."

"It's Thanksgiving this week. I think that will be celebration enough."

"You do keep bragging about your pecan pie."

"I do not *brag* about it."

Gavin settled behind the wheel, more happiness and harmony in his heart than he'd ever had. "You're coming out to cook at the ranch, right?"

"My place is way too small," she said, studying the side of his face as he drove. "It's still okay, isn't it?"

"'Course. And we'll come on Friday too. Visit my grandparents."

"You can leave the ranch?"

"Cruz will take care of the ranch for a few days."

"Ooh, look at you, all fancy with your cowboy employees."

Gavin's chest swelled with a bit of pride. He hadn't anticipated how much work the ranch would be, and he'd relied a lot on Jake, the previous owner of the ranch who still lived just down the lane. Cruz and Bowen were cowhands who had come with the ranch, and Gavin had relied on them a lot too.

"His family is coming here," he said. "Remember?"

"I remember. They're sleeping in your basement and we're feeding them turkey and cranberry sauce."

"And mashed potatoes. Cruz said his grandmother has never had mashed potatoes."

"I won't mess them up." Navy criss-crossed her heart and giggled. "I still can't believe she's never had them."

They went into the church, took their usual seat. Gavin was used to the staring, to people watching him and whispering about him. It had happened a lot in Three Rivers too, especially during his fifteen minutes of fame after saving Navy. The talk had mostly died now, but since Navy had come to town, it had revived.

Pastor Nye spoke about being grateful this holiday season, and Gavin's heart swelled. He had so much to be grateful for. So much had changed this year, and he scarcely recognized himself and his life from this time last year.

Lost as he was inside his own mind, it took him several minutes to realize Navy was weeping. When he did, he leaned down and cradled her close to his chest. "What's wrong?"

She shook her head and buried her face against him. He enjoyed the closeness he felt with her, and he couldn't wait until June so they could get married and experience this closeness all the time.

He let her cry through the end of the sermon and he bustled her out of the chapel so she wouldn't be embarrassed. Once in the safety of the truck, he turned to her. "What's going on? Are you all right?"

She looked at him with those beautiful eyes, tear-stained as they were. "I finally figured out how to forgive myself."

Emotion overcame him, and hot tears pricked his eyes too. "That's great, sweetheart."

She reached up and ran her fingers down the sides of his face as if seeing him for the first time. "I love you."

"And I love you."

She stretched up to kiss him, and Gavin received her gladly. His desire for her never seemed to lessen, something for which he would be grateful for until the end of his days.

# Seven Months Later

Gavin paced in his office, which had been set up as a staging room for him, the groom. He stared at the framed ticket to Three Rivers Navy had hung beside the door the previous afternoon.

He traced his fingers around the edge of the frame, looking at the date on the ticket. The date she'd come back to him. The date he'd always remember as the time he'd stopped being so angry about the legends and myths surrounding the town where he'd spent his whole life.

"You're still in there, right?" Grandmother's voice came through the closed door.

"Yes, Grandmother."

"Granddad is coming. Don't come out until we say. Navy doesn't want you to see the dress until she's walking down the aisle."

More foolish traditions, in Gavin's opinion, but if she

didn't want him to see her dress, he wouldn't see it. He loved her, romantic fantasies and all.

"We're almost ready," Grandmother said. He'd given up the master bedroom for Navy, and she was currently shut in there with her mother, her sister, and her best friend Lynn. He was sure Grandmother was about to join them.

He'd been entertaining Navy's family for three days already, and he was ready for this shindig to be over and done. Then they'd all go home. He and Navy would take their honeymoon to Hawaii, and when they returned to the ranch, she'd be here permanently.

She'd already moved all her stuff into the house. She'd been living out of a suitcase in a hotel room for two days. Her family had been staying in his basement, and Gavin had heard more about Navy than he wanted to know. Her sister talked incessantly, and her mother seemed to agree with everything Lexie said.

He could no longer fault Navy for not getting along with them very well. Her brother and father were much more tolerable, as John seemed genuinely interested in what Gavin did on the ranch. He asked questions about the horses and the cattle, which they'd taken out to the wild land a couple of months ago. Noah, her father, helped around the house, and he kept Gavin company in the evenings. Yes, Gavin rather liked both of them.

Granddad slipped into the room. "Your parents are almost here," he said in his raspy voice. Relief pulled through Gavin. He wasn't sure his parents would make it with the storms on the east coast canceling over a hundred flights. They still hadn't met Navy, and Gavin's relief rushed out of him in favor of panic.

He let Granddad hand him his boots and say, "You seem nervous, son."

"I'm getting married today," Gavin said, his voice edged with frustration that he tried to tame. "And I've been here before when the bride didn't show up."

Granddad nodded and smiled. "She's here, Gavin." He brushed something invisible from Gavin's ultra-black tuxedo and turned. "Your grandmother and I have a gift."

"Oh, no, you didn't have to."

"Of course we did. You cared for us for so long, put your dreams on hold." Granddad teared up and his voice sounded somewhat squeaky. "We're so happy for you." He extended a long box toward Gavin, who took it.

"Granddad."

"It was my father's. He wore it on his wedding day, and I wore it on mine. Even your father wore it."

A sense of reverence filled the office, and Gavin lifted the lid of the box in slow motion. Inside, white tissue paper concealed the gift, and he carefully moved it. A piercing blue tie sat inside, a crest embroidered on the bottom. The crest contained a delicate R intertwined with ivy and flowers, and Gavin's breath hitched.

"You're a Redd," Granddad said. "Remember that you represent more than just you. You wear our name."

Gavin gathered his granddad into a hug, his heart clogging his throat. "Thanks, Granddad." He allowed Granddad to put the tie on and fix the knot, his gnarled hands shaking by the time he finished.

The door burst open, and in blew his father. Gavin's chest cinched and then released at the large presence. "Dad."

His dad embraced him, bringing with him the scent of musk and leather, and clapped him on the back. "We just met Navy." He held Gavin by the shoulders. "She's wonderful." He beamed at his son, and all of Gavin's fears evaporated.

"Thanks, Dad."

"Hey, Dad." His father embraced his own father, and Grandmother poked her white-haired head into the office. "Gavin, you better get in position."

He nodded and he left the office first, the other men in his family behind him. He glanced toward the master bedroom, but the door remained securely closed. His heart kicked out an extra beat at the thought of his bride being so close.

The heat hit him full in the face when he left the homestead, and sweat formed under the brim of his cowboy hat. He strode out to the yard where Navy had selected the flattest part of the yard where they would be married. A trellis and several tents had been set up, along with fans and misters. Most of the chairs were already full, and Pastor Nye worked the crowd in his infectious way.

"Ah, there he is," the preacher boomed. "Our groom." He slung his arm around Gavin's shoulders. "You ready for this?"

Though the rehearsal had just been the previous evening, Gavin still felt miles out of his league. "Yes, sir," he managed to tell Pastor Nye, and they made their way to the front of the crowd.

"You stand here," the pastor said. "And I'll be here." He looked down the aisle where Navy would walk, and Gavin followed his gaze. The walkway seemed impossibly long and narrow, making his nerves dance a little faster.

There was no organist, but sweet and simple piano music wafted from the speakers set in the corners of the structures. Gavin swallowed; his parents and grandparents took their seats; so did Navy's mother and her siblings. Only Navy's father remained near the homestead.

Finally, she emerged from the house, and Gavin stared. Stared at the miles and miles of white fabric. Stared at the curves of her body. Stared at her beautiful face.

He couldn't believe she was going to be his. His heart pounded and hammered and tried to leap from his chest. Someone switched the piano music to the wedding march, and Navy stepped onto the walkway, her hand in her father's elbow.

He blinked and she stood beside him. He reached for her hand, and she willingly gave it to him. Willingly gave herself to him. Gratitude and love flowed from him to her as their vows were read, as Pastor Nye united them as husband and wife, as he leaned down and kissed her—the first kiss of the rest of his life.

Navy tilted her head back and laughed. She turned toward the crowd and lifted their joined hands. Gavin grinned, the fear of being abandoned finally, finally gone.

The crowd cheered, and hugs were given out to family members. Even Steve hugged him and Navy. Gavin let himself get washed away in all the festivities. The dinner. The dancing. And when he finally got his wife alone, he kissed her, and held her close to his heart, and whispered, "I love you, Navy."

And the best part was she did all the same things for him too, and Gavin silently thanked the Lord for her in his life. He may have also issued a bit of gratitude to the legend of that fountain in Three Rivers, Texas that had brought Navy all the way from Dallas and into his life.

* * *

Keep reading for a sneak peek of the next book in the Three Rivers Ranch Romance™ series, **Sixteen Steps to Fall in Love**.

# Sneak Peek! Sixteen Steps to Fall in Love Chapter One

Boone Carver yawned and stretched from his perch on the edge of his bed. From the other room, dog collars jingled and jangled as his bulldog and his yellow lab heard him and came running.

"Hey, guys." Amidst slobber from Lord Vader's jowls and tail whipping from Princess Leia's overactive rump, Boone scrubbed down the dogs. "You ready to run this morning?"

Of course they were. His dogs loved running almost as much as Boone did. The Annual Amarillo Marathon was only eight short months away, and he was determined to be ready this year. His muscles ached a bit from his long run yesterday, coupled with the late shift at the animal clinic where he worked. They stayed open until eight on Thursdays, and while that didn't normally faze Boone, the five a.m. alarm to put in ten miles before breakfast did.

He reminded himself that it was almost the weekend and he didn't have to work this one. He would be on call, but most people didn't call into the shelter unless there was a real emergency.

Dressed, stretched, and properly hydrated, Boone set out with Vader and Leia leashed beside him. Leia always tried to bolt out of the gate, and he had to hold her back, save some of his energy for mile six, when the fatigue would really hit him.

Boone lived on the northeast edge of Three Rivers, one of the last houses before the road stretched and went out to Three Rivers Ranch, where he worked part-time.

He timed his breathing, measured his steps, and enjoyed the early summer morning air. It smelled like apples and pollen, and Boone relished in this town, this place he'd come to find sanctuary at a time he'd had none.

He passed an older gentleman walking a Boston terrier, and Boone lifted his hand in greeting. He'd seen that dog in the clinic a few months ago. Cracked paw pads. Looked like the dog had fully healed, and Boone's spirits soared. With his mind on work, he ran through the late-night paperwork he'd completed.

He'd gone over it three times, determined not to give any more ammunition to the office administrator who'd been in his face since the day he'd arrived at the clinic. If his handwriting wasn't "atrocious" and "illegible" then he'd forgotten to check some microscopic box on the sixteenth line on page three of a form. If not that, then he'd misspelled something so important Nicole Hymas had to tell the entire staff of his incompetence.

He'd laughed it off all while shooting her his most lasered looks. Over the past several months, though, he'd decided to make more of an effort to hide his dyslexic tendencies. Last night, he'd even erased an entire paragraph and rewritten it so she'd be able to read it more easily.

He wasn't sure why Nicole disliked him so much. Messy handwriting came with the territory of a doctor, right?

*Yes, definitely*, he told himself as he hit the Six-Mile Wall. Thankfully, he spent part of his time out at Three Rivers, so he didn't have to deal with Nicole and her surliness on Mondays or Wednesdays.

He approached the end of his run: a huge park, with public restrooms, statues, a fountain everyone threw coins in to make wishes, and a bark park—a fenced area just for the pooches. He pulled out the pop up bowl for his dogs and filled it with water. Lord Vader and Princess Leia drank greedily while Boone stretched and worked out the lactic acid in his muscles.

His running route on ten-mile days took him around Three Rivers and always ended at this park. When the dogs had finished lapping at several bowls of water, he walked them over to the bark park, scanning the area now that the sun had painted the surroundings in golden rays of light.

Only a handful of people came to the park this early, and Boone knew almost all of them. He nodded and waved and smiled before opening the gate and unleashing his dogs. They'd just run for a while, but Boone liked this cooling down period at the pet park. Enjoyed talking to the people who shared his love of animals. Had even met his hiking partner and Friday night, game-watching best friend, Luke Morris, at this park.

Almost everyone in town knew he what he did for a living, and he often answered questions while he rubbed out his calves and rehydrated for the day.

Today, no one approached him, and he ripped open a protein bar from his backpack. Leia scampered around with a little pug he'd never seen before, and he glanced around for the dog's owner.

It had to be the copper-haired woman with her back to him. More the color of a tarnished penny, one that had seen a lot of days in the dirt, her hair still reminded him a bit of his aunt's. This woman was bent over another dog, her hair loose and flowing in a curtain that hid her face.

She picked up the tiny dog she'd been ministering to and straightened, scanning the park for the little pug. She wore a pair of tight yoga pants over her petite frame, along with an oversized sweatshirt in the exact shade of purple that reminded him of the grapes that grew on his family's ranch down in Hill Country.

His heart pounded out the promise that she'd be his next date. He hadn't been out with a woman in a couple of months, having decided not to burn through all the available females in the town in under a year.

He'd been in Three Rivers now for twelve months and five days, and he thought he'd like to get to know this woman a little better. Maybe a lot better.

"Taz," she called, turning toward him.

Boone startled, and promptly told his pulse to settle back into its proper place. *Now*.

Because the owner of the pug was none other than Nicole Hymas, the office administrator at the animal clinic where he worked three days a week.

He sucked in a breath when her eyes landed on his. She froze too, her surprise quickly melting into the usual sour expression she wore whenever she looked at Boone.

"He's over there." He indicated where the fawn-colored pug played with Leia.

Nicole frowned as she followed his hand gesture. She carried a tiny apricot-colored poodle that quivered in her arms as she stepped closer and closer to where Boone stood, his bulldog panting at his feet.

"Is this your dog?" She indicated Lord Vader.

"And that one playing with yours. Taz, is it?" Boone had never interacted with Nicole in such a civil way. He didn't even know the woman came in packaging labeled "nice." She'd been nasty to him since day one, and he'd never known why. But now, he smelled something like mint and lemons, and she didn't have any tension in her face, and her eyes didn't look like they were about to scald him.

"Yes." She beamed down at the little dog in her arms. "And this is Valcor."

Boone laughed, the sound flying free up toward the clouds. "That doesn't seem to fit."

Nicole scowled, effectively silencing Boone's clumsy laugh. "Thanks." She strode back to where she'd been standing and retrieved a small pack, which she buckled around her waist. Boone tried not to notice how trim she was—how had he missed it before? He tried not to stare at the way her hair nearly reached the pack—how had he never known she possessed yards of such beautiful hair?

She tossed him a disgruntled look he was very familiar with before leashing the pug and leaving the bark park. Boone watched her go, dateless and wondering if he could ever do anything right in the woman's eyes.

* * *

Boone arrived at Paw Pals Animal Clinic a few minutes before nine, already tired and hoping Nicole had called in sick.

No such luck. The woman sat in her office, which bore a large window that overlooked the lobby area, where a receptionist greeted customers when they arrived.

"Good morning, Boone," Joanne chirped, drawing

Nicole's attention. She rolled her eyes and Boone wished he possessed a superpower that could melt glass.

"Morning," he said, moving past the reception desk and through the door where he'd bring dogs to be treated. He had an office too, thank you very much. No window facing the facilities, so he entered and closed the door behind him, giving himself the privacy he wanted. Emerald green grass stretched beyond the window facing the outdoors, and Boone wished he were out there instead of in here.

He sighed, recalling the fantasy. He loved his job. He just didn't love working with Nicole. Heck, he'd appreciate it if he even *liked* working with Nicole. And now his blunder at the bark park had added fuel to an already simmering fire.

"But Valcor is a really odd name for a five-pound poodle," he muttered to himself as he put his lunch in the mini-fridge in the corner. He'd see all the dogs and cats that came in today, and he always checked the animals in the shelter on Fridays as well.

He turned away from the window at the faint sound of a woman singing. Nicole. She walked around the clinic with lyrics under her breath or a hum in the back of her throat. Boone had never minded—until today. Now, the sound of her voice sent his nerves across a cheese grater.

*Be nice*, he coached himself as he shrugged into his lab coat and exited his office to take the sixteen steps out to the reception area to get the chart for his first pet—and where he'd see Nicole. *Be nice, be nice, be nice....*

$$* * *$$

A cowboy who works sixteen steps from the woman of his dreams...and doesn't even know she's there. Can a chance meeting in a different location open his eyes to a chance at love?

**Look for SIXTEEN STEPS TO FALL IN LOVE
by scanning the QR code below!**

**Second Chance Ranch: A Three Rivers Ranch Romance™ (Book 1):** After his deployment, injured and discharged Major Squire Ackerman returns to Three Rivers Ranch, wanting to forgive Kelly for ignoring him a decade ago. He'd like to provide the stable life she needs, but with old wounds opening and a ranch on the brink of financial collapse, it will take patience and faith to make their second chance possible.

**Third Time's the Charm: A Three Rivers Ranch Romance™ (Book 2):** First Lieutenant Peter Marshall has a truckload of debt and no way to provide for a family, but Chelsea helps him see past all the obstacles, all the scars. With so many unknowns, can Pete and Chelsea develop the love, acceptance, and faith needed to find their happily ever after?

**Fourth and Long: A Three Rivers Ranch Romance™ (Book 3):** Commander Brett Murphy goes to Three Rivers Ranch to find some rest and relaxation with his Army buddies. Having his ex-wife show up with a seven-year-old she claims is his son is anything but the R&R he craves. Kate needs to make amends, and Brett needs to find forgiveness, but are they too late to find their happily ever after?

**Fifth Generation Cowboy: A Three Rivers Ranch Romance™ (Book 4):** Tom Lovell has watched his friends find their true happiness on Three Rivers Ranch, but everywhere he looks, he only sees friends. Rose Reyes has been bringing her daughter out to the ranch for equine therapy for months, but it doesn't seem to be working. Her challenges with Mari are just as frustrating as ever. Could Tom be exactly what Rose needs? Can he remove his friendship blinders and find love with someone who's been right in front of him all this time?

**Sixth Street Love Affair: A Three Rivers Ranch Romance™ (Book 5):** After losing his wife a few years back, Garth Ahlstrom thinks he's ready for a second chance at love. But Juliette Thompson has a secret that could destroy their budding relationship. Can they find the strength, patience, and faith to make things work?

**The Seventh Sergeant: A Three Rivers Ranch Romance™ (Book 6):** Life has finally started to settle down for Sergeant Reese Sanders after his devastating injury overseas. Discharged from the Army and now with a good job at Courage Reins, he's finally found happiness—until a horrific fall puts him right back where he was years ago: Injured and depressed. Carly Watters, Reese's new veteran care coordinator, dislikes small towns almost as much as she loathes cowboys. But she finds herself faced with both when she gets assigned to Reese's case. Do they have the humility and faith to make their relationship more than professional?

**Eight Second Ride: A Three Rivers Ranch Romance™ (Book 7):** Ethan Greene loves his work at Three Rivers Ranch, but he can't seem to find the right woman to settle down with. When sassy yet vulnerable Brynn Bowman shows up at the ranch to recruit him back to the rodeo circuit, he takes a different approach with the barrel racing champion. His patience and newfound faith pay off when a friendship--and more--starts with Brynn. But she wants out of the rodeo circuit right when Ethan wants to rejoin. Can they find the path God wants them to take and still stay together?

**The Ninth Inning: A Three Rivers Ranch Romance™ (Book 8):** The Christmas season has never felt like such a burden to boutique owner Andrea Larsen. But with Mama gone and the holidays upon her, Andy finds herself wishing she hadn't been so quick to judge her former boyfriend, cowboy Lawrence Collins. Well, Lawrence hasn't forgotten about Andy either, and he devises a plan to get her out to the ranch so they can reconnect. Do they have the faith and humility to patch things up and start a new relationship?

**Ten Days in Town: A Three Rivers Ranch Romance™ (Book 9):** Sandy Keller is tired of the dating scene in Three Rivers. Though she owns the pancake house, she's looking for a fresh start, which means an escape from the town where she grew up. When her older brother's best friend, Tad Jorgensen, comes to town for the holidays, it is a balm to his weary soul. A helicopter tour guide who experienced a near-death experience, he's looking to start over too--but in Three Rivers. Can Sandy and Tad navigate their troubles to find the path God wants them to take--and discover true love--in only ten days?

**Eleven Year Reunion: A Three Rivers Ranch Romance™ (Book 10):** Pastry chef extraordinaire, Grace Lewis has moved to Three Rivers to help Heidi Ackerman open a bakery in Three Rivers. Grace relishes the idea of starting over in a town where no one knows about her failed cupcakery. She doesn't expect to run into her old high school boyfriend, Jonathan Carver. A carpenter working at Three Rivers Ranch, Jon's in town against his will. But with Grace now on the scene, Jon's thinking life in Three Rivers is suddenly looking up. But with her focus on baking and his disdain for small towns, can they make their eleven year reunion stick?

**The Twelfth Town: A Three Rivers Ranch Romance™ (Book 11):** Newscaster Taryn Tucker has had enough of life on-screen. She's bounced from town to town before arriving in Three Rivers, completely alone and completely anonymous--just the way she now likes it. She takes a job cleaning at Three Rivers Ranch, hoping for a chance to figure out who she is and where God wants her. When she meets happy-go-lucky cowhand Kenny Stockton, she doesn't expect sparks to fly. Kenny's always been "the best friend" for his female friends, but the pull between him and Taryn can't be denied. Will they have the courage and faith necessary to make their opposite worlds mesh?

**Lucky Number Thirteen: A Three Rivers Ranch Romance™ (Book 12):** Tanner Wolf, a rodeo champion ten times over, is excited to be riding in Three Rivers for the first time since he left his philandering ways and found religion. Seeing his old friends Ethan and Brynn is therapuetic--until a terrible accident lands him in the hospital. With his rodeo career over, Tanner thinks maybe he'll stay in town--and it's not just because his nurse, Summer Hamblin, is the prettiest woman he's ever met. But Summer's the queen of first dates, and as she looks for a way to make a relationship with the transient rodeo star work Summer's not sure she has the fortitude to go on a second date. Can they find love among the tragedy?

**The Curse of February Fourteenth: A Three Rivers Ranch Romance™ (Book 13):** Cal Hodgkins, cowboy veterinarian at Bowman's Breeds, isn't planning to meet anyone at the masked dance in small-town Three Rivers. He just wants to get his bachelor friends off his back and sit on the sidelines to drink his punch. But when he sees a woman dressed in gorgeous butterfly wings and cowgirl boots with blue stitching, he's smitten. Too bad she runs away from the dance before he can get her name, leaving only her boot behind...

**Fifteen Minutes of Fame: A Three Rivers Ranch Romance™ (Book 14):** Navy Richards is thirty-five years of tired—tired of dating the same men, working a demanding job, and getting her heart broken over and over again. Her aunt has always spoken highly of the matchmaker in Three Rivers, Texas, so she takes a six-month sabbatical from her high-stress job as a pediatric nurse, hops on a bus, and meets with the matchmaker. Then she meets Gavin Redd. He's handsome, he's hardworking, and he's a cowboy. But is he an Aquarius too? Navy's not making a move until she knows for sure...

**Sixteen Steps to Fall in Love: A Three Rivers Ranch Romance™ (Book 15):** A chance encounter at a dog park sheds new light on the tall, talented Boone that Nicole can't ignore. As they get to know each other better and start to dig into each other's past, Nicole is the one who wants to run. This time from her growing admiration and attachment to Boone. From her aging parents. From herself.

But Boone feels the attraction between them too, and he decides he's tired of running and ready to make Three Rivers his permanent home. **Can Boone and Nicole use their faith to overcome their differences and find a happily-ever-after together?**

**The Sleigh on Seventeenth Street: A Three Rivers Ranch Romance™ (Book 16):** A cowboy with skills as an electrician tries a relationship with a down-on-her luck plumber. Can Dylan and Camila make water and electricity play nicely together this Christmas season? Or will they get shocked as they try to make their relationship work?

**The First Lady of Three Rivers Ranch: A Three Rivers Ranch Romance™ (Book 17):** Heidi Duffin has been dreaming about opening her own bakery since she was thirteen years old. She scrimped and saved for years to afford baking and pastry school in San Francisco. And now she only has one year left before she's a certified pastry chef. Frank Ackerman's father has recently retired, and he's taken over the largest cattle ranch in the Texas Panhandle. A horseman through and through, he's also nearing thirty-one and looking for someone to bring love and joy to a homestead that's been dominated by men for a decade. But when he convinces Heidi to come clean the cowboy cabins, she changes all that. But the siren's call of a bakery is still loud in Heidi's ears, even if she's also seeing a future with Frank. Can she rely on her faith in ways she's never had to before or will their relationship end when summer does?

# Second Generation in Three Rivers Romance™ Series

Step back into the heartwarming small Texas town of Three Rivers! This beloved town has captured the hearts of 2.5 million readers and caught the eye of Sony Pictures, and now a new generation of cowboys and cowgirls is ready to take center stage. Scan the QR code below with your phone to check out this new series!

1. The Cowboy Who Came Home - featuring Squire's son, Finn from SECOND CHANCE RANCH!

# Seven Sons Ranch in Three Rivers Romance™ Series

Meet the cowboy billionaire brothers at Seven Sons Ranch! Scan the QR code below with your phone to check out this complete series.

1. Rhett
2. Tripp
3. Liam
4. Jeremiah
5. Wyatt
6. Skyler
7. Micah
8. Gideon

# Shiloh Ridge Ranch in Three Rivers Romance™ Series

Meet the cowboy billionaires in the southern hills outside of Three Rivers! Scan the QR code below with your phone to check out this complete series.

1. The Mechanics of Mistletoe
2. The Horsepower of the Holiday
3. The Construction of Cheer
4. The Secret of Santa
5. The Gift of Gingerbread
6. The Harmony of Holly
7. The Chemistry of Christmas
8. The Delivery of Decor
9. The Blessing of Babies
10. The Networking of the Nativity
11. The Wrangling of the Wreath
12. The Hope of Her Heart

# About Liz

Liz Isaacson writes inspirational romance, usually set in Texas, or Wyoming, or anywhere else horses and cowboys exist. She lives in Utah, where she writes full-time, takes her two dogs to the park everyday, and eats a lot of veggies while writing. Find her on her website at feelgoodfiction-books.com